Conlon opened
wouldn't com...

Glorianna looked ... ... minute, he lost himself in her eyes. He reached up and wrapped a strand of her silky hair around his fingers. The burnished red gleamed in the first rays of sunlight.

He tried again. "How will you know when you've found the right husband?" His voice sounded raspy with emotion. He held his breath, waiting for what seemed an eternity for her answer.

Glorianna pulled her hand free from his, leaving his fingers empty. She reached slowly up and softly brushed a stray lock of hair back from his forehead. "I'll know," she whispered.

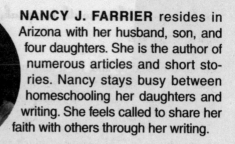

NANCY J. FARRIER resides in Arizona with her husband, son, and four daughters. She is the author of numerous articles and short stories. Nancy stays busy between homeschooling her daughters and writing. She feels called to share her faith with others through her writing.

Sonoran Sunrise

Nancy J. Farrier

Heartsong Presents

To my Savior, Jesus Christ, Who has blessed me so richly.

To my parents, John and Ruth, who took the time to read to me, and passed on their love of books.

A note from the author:
I love to hear from my readers! You may correspond with me by writing: Nancy J. Farrier
                                             Author Relations
                                             PO Box 719
                                             Uhrichsville, OH 44683

ISBN 1-58660-154-7

SONORAN SUNRISE

All of the characters and events in this book are fictitious. Any resemblance to actual persons, living or dead, or to actual events is purely coincidental.

Cover illustration by Dominick Saponaro.

one

Camp MacDowell, Arizona Territory—1870s

"Daddy, how could you do this to me?" The petite young woman stalked through the open door, her rust-colored dress and parasol leaving a trail of travel dust.

Lieutenant Conlon Sullivan watched in amusement as the normally stern Captain Richard Wilton lost his military composure in the face of the fiery redhead's anger. Conlon knew this must be Glorianna Wilton, the captain's daughter, newly arrived at Camp MacDowell, Arizona Territory.

"I'm sorry, Sir." A red-faced orderly stood behind the young woman wringing his hands. "I tried to stop her."

Captain Wilton's mouth snapped closed and he waved a hand at the orderly who stumbled over his feet as he backed from the room and pulled the door shut behind him.

"Daddy, I can't believe you would make me come to this horrible country to live. Do you hate me this much?" Jewel green eyes sparkled with fire. "There isn't even a decent road for miles. I've been bumped and jolted for days. Not to mention the abysmal boat trip up the Colorado River to get to Arizona Territory."

Captain Wilton stood and rounded the desk in record time. "Kitten, I didn't want to upset you, but I needed to see you." He tried to draw her into his arms, but the girl withdrew a step and stiffened her slender back.

Conlon watched in silence as Captain Wilton regained his composure. *Hmm. Anger doesn't appear to be working. I wonder if she'll try pleading now—or tears.*

"I'm sorry. I know the trip out here is strenuous. I thought it best, after your mother died, to bring you here to be with me."

5

Biting his lower lip to stifle his laughter, Conlon watched the rigidity melt from the girl. Her face took on a lost puppy look. *She's good,* he thought. *I'll bet she's used to wrapping him around her finger. Still, her wiles may not work now that she's grown.*

Taking advantage of the momentary lull, Conlon studied the captain's daughter. Her once shining dress, now travel-stained and dusty, covered a willowy figure. A crumpled, yet stylish hat sat askew on a head of the brightest red hair he had seen since leaving home. She reminded him of his mother with her fiery hair and temper. His fingers twitched as he longed to reach out and brush a strand of hair from her silky white cheek, wanting to know if her skin and hair were as soft as they appeared.

"I'm sorry, Daddy." Her apology broke the silence. "I wanted to see you, too. I just didn't realize the trip here would be so gruesome."

"Hey, Kitten." Richard Wilton lifted his daughter's chin with a gentle finger. "I didn't consider how difficult the journey would be for you. Now that you're here I'm sure you'll love Arizona."

Shoulders slumped, she gazed up at her father. "Daddy, I must return home. Please. This was the worst time for me to come. You don't understand."

Captain Wilton's brows drew together in a puzzled frown as he looked down at his beautiful daughter. "Why do you want to go back to Boston?"

"Oh, Daddy, I have to get back to Kendrick. You remember Kendrick Hanford, don't you?" She reached out to brush a piece of lint from her father's cavalry jacket.

Captain Wilton's frown deepened. "Of course, I remember the Hanford boy. If I recall, he's the one who tipped over outhouses and threw rotten eggs at any likely target—including me. What about him?"

The young woman's cheeks reddened and her green eyes twinkled. "Oh, Daddy, he was just a boy when he did those things. Now he's a responsible young man, and I intend to marry him."

I suspect the tears will appear any second now. Conlon struggled to suppress a smile. *She's just like my sister Maria.*

"Marry him?" Captain Wilton questioned. "Has he declared his intentions?"

"Well, not exactly," she said as she twirled her dainty parasol, sending a dust shower to the floor. "But, I know he will, Daddy." She laid a slender hand on his shirtfront, her eyes bright with unshed tears. Like a drop of honey, a single tear traced a path down her cheek. "Daddy, I'm almost an old maid. In four months I'll be eighteen. I have to get married now."

Conlon almost laughed aloud at the thought of this vision's being an old maid. The slender beauty certainly didn't look the part. *Lord, I do believe she's an answer to my prayers.* At that moment, Conlon Sullivan knew without a doubt he would marry the captain's daughter. Softly, he cleared his throat.

Cat green eyes locked on his and a soft rose blush crept up her apple blossom cheeks. Captain Wilton looked momentarily confused before his commanding demeanor returned. "Pardon me, Sullivan. I seem to have forgotten my manners." He gestured at his daughter. "Allow me to introduce you to my daughter, Glorianna. Glorianna, this is Lieutenant Conlon Sullivan."

She brushed the stray strands of hair out of her face and back into place, her eyes never leaving Conlon's face. "I'm pleased to meet you." Her lilting voice turned soft with almost a musical quality to it.

Conlon didn't think he would ever breathe again. This enchanting woman stole his every thought. Her heart-shaped face, like that of the angel on his mother's Christmas tree, captivated him. Moments passed. Suddenly, he realized they were staring at him. "Pleased," he stammered like an untried boy. Then, regaining a measure of his usual confidence, he continued. "I'm pleased to meet you, Miss Wilton. We don't usually have the privilege of such pleasant company in the middle of the desert."

Glorianna inspected the handsome cavalry lieutenant facing her. Laughing blue eyes, deep set beside a slightly crooked nose, started her heart tripping faster than normal. Even, white teeth lit up a face tanned from hours in the sun. Neatly combed coal black hair lay straight, except for one wayward shock hanging down on his forehead.

What would it be like to tuck that lock of hair back into place? she wondered. The thought of being that close to such a commanding, strong-muscled man took her breath away. *What is wrong with me? I want to marry Kendrick, yet here I am attracted to the first man I meet in Arizona.*

"I'm sure it would be okay for you to wait outside, Lieutenant, while I finish talking with my father." Glorianna knew she had to get this man out of here. "Isn't that right, Daddy?"

Captain Wilton frowned, then turned to Conlon. "Please excuse us, Lieutenant. Wait outside, though. I'll have you escort Glorianna to our quarters in a moment."

"But, Daddy, I thought you would show me around."

"I'd love to, Kitten, but I have a lot of work to finish here. Lieutenant Sullivan is perfectly capable."

Conlon flashed a smile at her as he walked out of the office. Glorianna tried hard to be angry at his obvious pleasure in being assigned to escort her. *He just doesn't know how much I love Kendrick,* she thought. *He'll give up soon.*

"Daddy," she said, turning to see her father once again standing behind his desk.

"Now, Glorianna, don't start. You just arrived. Give Arizona a chance. You might like it better than Boston."

"Daddy, it has nothing to do with Boston or Arizona. I have to marry Kendrick. Every girl in Boston wants to be his wife. If I don't get back right away, he might just agree to marry one of them."

"Well, if that's the case, then perhaps he isn't the right man for you anyway," Richard Wilton suggested.

Twirling her parasol again, Glorianna noted the cloud of dust drifting from its folds and she shook free the rest of the travel dirt. "Daddy, it isn't just Kendrick."

"Then have a seat and tell me what it is."

Glorianna sank into the chair vacated by Conlon as her father dropped heavily into his desk chair. "Oh, Daddy, I've dreamed of marrying Kendrick and living in a cottage, just the two of us. I want a little cottage with a white picket fence. The neighbor ladies could open the little gate when they come to visit. We could sit outside and drink tea among the rose bushes while we listen to the birds sing." Glorianna heard the wistful note in her voice and shook herself back to reality. "Now do you understand?"

Richard Wilton's eyes shone with tears and he watched his daughter a moment before speaking. "You look and sound so much like your mother, Kitten. I could almost believe she was sitting across from me." He stopped to clear the huskiness from his throat. "I believe I understand, but I just can't let you leave yet. You'll have to at least wait until a company is traveling across to the Colorado River. Right now, I can't spare the men necessary to escort you. Besides, I expect to receive new orders by Christmas. It's possible I'll be sent back east."

"Christmas!" Glorianna stiffened in anger. "Christmas is months away, and by then it could be too late."

"I'm sorry, Glorianna, but that's the way it is." Captain Wilton rose from his desk, stepped around, and took her arm. "Now come on. I'll have Lieutenant Sullivan show you to our quarters and he can introduce you to some of our neighbors."

Smiling at his daughter, he continued. "Maybe it won't be so bad as you think. After all, you have no competition here and I'm sure you could find plenty of suitors."

"That's the last thing I want," Glorianna shot back. "I don't want to be married to an army man who will be traipsing off who knows where just when I need him."

As the words left her mouth, Glorianna wished she could

draw them back. She knew from the look on her father's face that she'd hurt him deeply. He couldn't help leaving her and her mother. The army was his job. You couldn't simply quit that kind of a job. He hadn't wanted to leave a sick wife and a young daughter, but he had had no choice.

"I'm sorry, Daddy," Glorianna said softly, gently touching his cheek. "You always did the best you could. Mother loved you so much."

Richard Wilton pulled her close, then said gruffly, "It's time for you to go. Lieutenant Sullivan!"

⁂

"These are the parade grounds," Conlon said, gesturing toward a large area of brown sand dotted with scraggly, unrecognizable plants. "Every morning we have our drills here and most everybody comes to watch." He grinned down at her, his bright smile lighting his face. "Here in the desert you take any excitement you can get."

Glorianna tried hard to contain her anger as Conlon Sullivan insisted on strolling slowly around the camp and pointing out the various sights before taking her by the officers' quarters. She simply had to get away from this man. His presence bothered her more than she cared to admit. She constantly found her gaze drifting to his arms. Even through the sleeves of his cavalry tunic, she could tell they were well muscled, and she kept wondering what it would feel like to be held by them.

"Would you please show me to my father's house, Lieutenant Sullivan?" She stiffened her resolve and tried hard to recall Kendrick's face, but only a pair of sparkling blue eyes set above a once-broken nose appeared. "I've had a long day, and I really need to refresh myself before the dinner hour." Glorianna knew she sounded like some haughty city girl, but she couldn't help herself. She needed to escape his presence.

"Oh, but Miss Wilton," Conlon took her hand and firmly tucked it in the crook of his elbow, "you'll want to meet your neighbors, and we haven't even seen John Smith's store."

When she looked up, his azure eyes bore into hers. "Then, too, I'm sure you'll want to know where to find the dining hall. You don't want to run all over the camp hunting for your dinner, do you?"

Morning glory blue, she decided. *His eyes look just like the morning glory climbing Mother's fence. The only difference is, his eyes still have the sparkle of the dew in them.* Shaking herself, she tugged, gently at first, then harder, trying to free her captive hand. "If we're going to finish this tour, Lieutenant, could we do it at a faster pace? And would you please release my hand?"

"I didn't realize you might be willing to run a race in this heat," Conlon said, barely holding his laughter in check. "I guess we can trot along, but I insist that I hold on to your hand. On this uneven ground, you could fall. I don't want to have to explain such an unfortunate accident to your father. Come then, let's step lively." Conlon started off once again, this time at a pace that took her breath away.

Much later, breathless and flushed, Glorianna marched past a row of officers' houses. The line of identical clapboard and adobe houses stood in formation, one after the other. She wanted to breathe a sigh of relief as Conlon paused before one of the copycat houses and knocked on a door.

"This is the home of Timothy and Fayth Holwell," Conlon stated, as he straightened his already erect military bearing. "I think you will like Fayth and, since you're next door neighbors, you should meet her first."

The door opened and a slender, dark-haired young woman peered out at them from the dim, cool interior of her house. "Conlon." Her face lit up with a sweet smile of welcome. "Do come in." She stepped to one side and Conlon slowly released Glorianna's hand so that she could precede him through the door.

Glorianna blinked her eyes to adjust after the brilliant sunshine outside. The inside of the house, surprisingly cool, exuded a homey atmosphere that put her at ease. A young girl toddled on unsteady legs across the uneven floor and hid her face in Fayth's skirt, peeking out to look at the visitors.

"Please sit down," Fayth said as she gestured to the few chairs grouped together at one side of the sparsely furnished room. "Conlon, what have you been doing to this young lady? Her face is as red as the sunset." Fayth called to someone in another room to bring drinks for them.

Conlon made the introductions. "She insisted we hurry our tour, Mrs. Holwell. I believe these Bostonians don't know how to move at the easier pace we Westerners are accustomed to."

"I certainly didn't intend to run a race, Lieutenant." Glorianna wished she could move her chair, for it sat much too close to Conlon's, and she could feel the heat of his gaze. She fought to avert her gaze lest she be captured once more by those eyes and find herself completely drawn to him.

Although she enjoyed the visit, Glorianna was relieved when she, at last, stood outside her door. "Thank you for the tour, Lieutenant Sullivan. I'm certain we shall cross paths again. It seems this is a rather small post."

An easy, heart-stopping smile swept over Conlon's face. "I'd say we'll cross paths again, Miss Wilton. After all, I heard you tell the captain about your dilemma. Since I'd hate to see such a beautiful woman become an old maid, I intend to ask your father's permission to court you."

two

Shock rendered her speechless. Glorianna stared at Conlon open-mouthed. Gently he placed one finger on her chin and pushed upward, closing her mouth. Then, with a cocky grin and a mock salute, he turned and strode toward the parade grounds.

"Never in my life have I been so insulted." Glorianna's words were spoken too late to reach the retreating Conlon. "I'll have a thing or two to say about this, Lieutenant Sullivan. You just wait and see."

Glorianna turned and stormed into the small house that she would share with her father. She ignored the crude furniture and the naked, hard-baked beige adobe walls. Instead, her thoughts were filled with Conlon's tanned and handsome face, which sported that arrogant smile and wayward lock of ebony hair.

Throughout the evening she found herself thinking of him. She tried to concentrate on Kendrick and how much she missed him. Strangely enough, she couldn't vividly recall his face. Her memory of him, already fading from the long trip to Arizona Territory, slipped even farther away, as if pushed by a certain rugged cavalry officer.

"Lieutenant Sullivan asked my permission to court you." Her father's voice jolted her out of her reverie. He looked at her over the top of a newspaper.

"I will not have him courting me," snapped Glorianna. "I plan to marry Kendrick when I go back east. There's no need of my being courted by anyone here."

Richard Wilton frowned. "You said the Hanford boy hasn't declared his intentions yet. Why is that?"

"Well," Glorianna shifted in her chair, "he's busy learning

13

his trade and probably wants to buy a house first."

"Exactly what is his trade? I seem to remember him as being rather shiftless."

"He is not shiftless." Glorianna's eyes flashed fire. "He's just trying out different positions to find the one that suits him best."

"Shiftless." Richard Wilton murmured, rustling his paper as he turned the page. From the depths of the wagon-train-carried, outdated newspaper, he stated, "I gave Sullivan my permission. He's smart, hardworking, and will make some woman a good husband. I think you'd do well to consider him."

Glorianna stood up stiffly, knowing when her father spoke in that tone there would be no changing his mind. "I believe I'll go on to bed. It's been a long day."

Tears of anger raced down her cheeks as she closed the door behind her. She threw herself on the bed, not caring about her already rumpled dress, nor about getting dirt on the bedclothes.

God, I know it's right for me to marry Kendrick. This is what I wanted so much. Why am I here when he's back there? I don't want to be courted by some cavalryman who will always be riding off to one battle or another. Glorianna buried her face in her covers and sobbed. She wondered if she would ever survive her father's edict.

❧

Conlon rose early, after a restless night filled with dreams of a red-haired girl with a freckled gumdrop nose. Walking through the predawn quiet, he left the camp to sit on a low rock. Every morning he liked to wait for the dawn and talk to God about the approaching day. This was his time to prepare and listen.

Thank You, God, for sending Glorianna here. He smiled, remembering the fiery beauty, longing to see her with that glorious chestnut hair hanging loose. Her flashing green eyes sparked with intelligence and a zest for life that he'd rarely seen in a woman.

Lord, I've waited a long time for a woman to share my dreams with and here she is. I want to marry her now. So, please help me to quickly convince her that I'm the one You've chosen for her.

As if in answer to his prayer, the sun peeked over the horizon at that moment. A dazzling array of pinks, yellows, and blues swept across the sky, taking Conlon's breath away with its beauty. *This must be God saying yes to me,* he thought as he pushed off the rock and headed back into the fort determined to win Glorianna's love.

❧

"Glorianna, can you come out here?" her father's voice cut through the fog of deep sleep.

Dragging herself slowly out of bed, Glorianna noted the sun, barely awake itself, was already warming the day. She hadn't slept well during the night and her eyes felt scratchy and heavy.

"I'll be right out."

Within minutes, Glorianna stepped out of her bedroom, wearing a fresh but travel-wrinkled dress, her hair neatly combed. "Good morning, Father," she said, as she stretched up to kiss his newly shaven cheek.

"Sorry to wake you, Kitten." Her father smiled. "This is an army post and we rise early. If you want breakfast you have to get up on time. Besides, I want you to meet someone." He turned toward his room and called, "Dirk, come here."

A man sidled into the room, his rounded shoulders hunching further as he faced the captain. His pockmarked face split into a wide grin at the sight of Glorianna.

In a flashing thought, she compared his blackened stubby teeth with a certain lieutenant's brilliant white smile. Dirk's hair, wet and dark from hair tonic, lay slicked back from a narrow face and hooked nose. Glorianna did her best to repress a shudder.

"Glorianna, this is Dirk Smith. He keeps house for us." Richard Wilton turned to his daughter. "I know it would be better for you to have a woman here. I've inquired, but so far I haven't found one. Until I do, Dirk will be taking care of us. This morning you'll eat in the dining hall, but after this Dirk will cook for us, too."

Dirk's dark gaze swept across Glorianna, making her squirm uncomfortably. She suppressed a shudder as his oily stare traveled over her. "It's nice to meet you, Mr. Smith," she said, trying to keep disgust from her voice. "I appreciate the help you give my father."

"Well, we'd better be off." Captain Wilton tugged his cap over his head. "We don't want to miss our breakfast."

Glorianna snapped open her parasol, shading herself from the sun even on the short walk to the mess hall. She hated the thought of more freckles popping out on her nose. They were such an embarrassment and impossible to get rid of once they appeared.

After breakfast, Glorianna's father headed to his office as she assured him that she would be fine unaccompanied on the short walk back to the house. Before she had gone two yards, Conlon Sullivan fell into step beside her, adjusting his long strides to match her shorter ones.

"Good morning, Miss Wilton."

Her cheeks warmed as his dazzling smile started her heart racing. "Good morning, Lieutenant Sullivan." She tried to take deep, slow breaths. "I'm sure you have other duties. I can find my way home just fine."

"Oh, but it's such a pleasure walking with you." His deep voice warmed her. She struggled between annoyance at his intrusion and her desire to hear him talk. "I guess your father told you that I spoke with him."

"Yes, he did." Glorianna stopped and faced Conlon. "I have to tell you, I intend to marry another man. Your attempts to court me will prove fruitless."

Conlon threw back his head and laughed aloud. Glorianna looked around furtively, hoping no one was watching them. "Please, Lieutenant Sullivan, I think you should give this up."

Tucking her hand in the crook of his arm, Conlon continued walking toward her house. "I don't intend to be turned away that easily, Miss Wilton. I believe God brought us together, and I intend to marry you."

Glorianna stopped suddenly and jerked her hand from Conlon's grasp. "Don't I have a say in this?" she asked as he turned to face her. "How dare you talk about our marriage as if you and God have already decided what's best for me."

Glorianna brushed past Conlon. Marching up to the nearest house, she knocked on the door.

Please be home, she thought. *I have to get away from him.*

A sigh of relief rushed from Glorianna's lips as Fayth Holwell opened the door. "Why, good morning, Glorianna." Fayth's face lit with a delighted smile. "I'm so glad you stopped by. Won't you come in?"

Fighting tears of anger, she brushed by Fayth to enter the cool house. "Good morning, Fayth. I hope you don't mind my visiting so early." Her voice trembled with a huskiness that belied her emotion. She could almost feel Conlon's lingering gaze as he watched her enter the house, but she refused to turn and look at him.

"Are you okay?" Fayth's sympathetic voice broke the dam which held Glorianna's tears at bay.

"I'm sorry, I didn't mean to come here and fall apart like this. I just had to get away from him."

"Away from Conlon Sullivan?" Fayth's voice registered her surprise. "Why, he's always such a gentleman."

"Maybe that's because you're a married woman." Glorianna didn't mean to sound so bitter.

"Did he do something improper?" Fayth eyes widened.

"No," Glorianna sighed. "He wasn't improper." For the next hour, Fayth listened as Glorianna explained how her father left her in charge of her invalid mother when he returned to his post out West. She told about seeing the other girls her age having fun when she couldn't and of feeling left out because she had to care for her mother. She spoke of her longing to belong to the group and how she wanted to be courted by the handsome and much sought-after Kendrick Hanford. Her voice softened as she described her longing to be married and live in a cottage surrounded by flowers and a picket fence.

"After Mother died, Father insisted I come out here. I tried to explain to him that I wanted to return to Boston right away, but he wouldn't listen." Glorianna shook her head and absently twirled her parasol. "Now he's given Lieutenant Sullivan permission to court me, despite my protests. Lieutenant Sullivan even had the audacity to tell me that he and God are in agreement that we should marry."

Fayth smiled and reached for Glorianna's hand. "Conlon is a good man. He's a little impatient, but if you give him a chance you might find yourself attracted to him. As for God. . . Well. . .He knows the plans He has for us. So, ask Him. I'm sure you'll find out in time what God wants for your life. Maybe you should even ask God what to look for in a husband."

"I guess you're right. I'll pray about the matter. But I'm sure God wants me to marry Kendrick." Glorianna lifted her head and looked around the neat room. "Meanwhile, is there something I can do to help you? I seem to have a lot of time on my hands, and I'm at a loss as to how to spend it."

Fayth gave a little laugh. "Have you any skill at sewing? I'm afraid I'm hopeless, and I'm trying to make a new dress for my daughter, Alyce."

"It just so happens I love to sew." Glorianna smiled in relief. "Let's get started."

&

The flames leaping out of the forge served to remind Conlon of the fiery hair and sparkling green eyes of Glorianna Wilton. The smooth rhythmic clanging of the blacksmith's hammer lulled him temporarily. Conlon recalled the gentle weight of her hand on his arm, and he longed to see her again. But, Glorianna didn't want to see him. He shook his head and sighed as he focused his attentions on his friend, Josiah Washington, the company's blacksmith.

"Mornin', Conlon," Josiah said as he dunked the red-hot horseshoe in a pail of water. The water hissed and a cloud of steam enveloped Josiah's sweating body.

"Good morning, Josiah. I came to see if you have Champ's shoes ready."

"I'm just finishing them." Josiah gestured to the horseshoe dripping water. "I'll fit him right away. Are you in a hurry?"

"No hurry." Conlon shook his head, trying to concentrate on his reason for being here.

"The boys said the captain's daughter arrived yesterday. Did you meet her yet?" Josiah's brows drew together as he watched Conlon. "What is the matter with you, anyway?"

Conlon couldn't hold back a grin. "You won't believe her, Josiah. God answered my prayers and sent me an angel to marry."

"You mean you're going to marry the captain's daughter?" Josiah looked incredulous. "Did you know her before?"

"I met her for the first time yesterday," Conlon admitted. "But, I know she's the one for me."

"And how does this angel feel about your marriage?"

Conlon frowned, "Well she is still a little wary of the idea."

"Uh-huh." Josiah nodded. "I've seen you do some things on the spur of the moment, but this might be too much. Don't you think you should get to know her a little first?"

"I already have the captain's permission to court her. We'll get to know each other faster that way. Besides, she wants to go back east and marry some man who isn't even interested in her. She just needs a little convincing to understand that I'm the right one for her."

Josiah shook his head and picked up the horseshoe. He examined it, frowned, and stuck it back in the coals of the forge. "Well, I'll pray for you, Conlon. Try not to get too pushy, though. You'll scare her off if you do."

❧

Glorianna smiled as she opened the door and slipped into her house. She'd had a wonderful morning with Fayth and her young daughter, Alyce. The dress, well on its way to being complete, would look darling on the little girl. It felt so nice to have another woman to talk to. Fayth loved God and talked of Him as if He was her best friend. She reminded Glorianna of her mother.

Crossing the living room to her bedroom, Glorianna intended to lie down for awhile. The rapidly warming day, coupled with the fact that she hadn't slept much last night, made her drowsy.

Stepping through the open door into her room, Glorianna paused and drew in a sharp breath. Dirk, hunched over her trunk, was pawing through her dresses and underthings.

"What are you doing?" Glorianna's sharp tone brought the man to his feet, his eyes darting around the room as if looking for a way to escape. "I asked what you're doing! Why are you going through my clothing?"

Dirk's pockmarked face split into a lecherous grin as his inky eyes traveled slowly over her. "Why, I'm just taking care of you like your father ordered, Miss Wilton. I thought I could put away some of your things for you."

"I can take care of my own clothes, Mr. Smith. You may leave now."

Glorianna tried not to cringe as he approached. When he paused beside her, she closed her eyes and clenched her teeth. *Please, God, get him out of here.*

A sigh of relief escaped her lips as he passed on out of the room.

three

Summer arrived with a vengeance. The days lengthened and the sun beat down unmercifully. Glorianna groaned as she dragged herself from bed after another sleepless night in her oven-hot room. Seated on the edge of her bed, she shook her head as she looked over her dresses. She couldn't bear the thought of putting on one of those snug-fitting dresses. The heavy material and tight bodices made her sweat, and her constricted breathing threatened to induce fainting spells.

"Glorianna?" Her father called from outside the door. "I need to talk to you before breakfast."

"I'll be right out." Glorianna reached for her amber colored dress. This one wasn't so formfitting. Perhaps she wouldn't be quite so miserable today.

"Good morning, Father." Glorianna gave him a quick kiss, trying to ignore Dirk as he worked at cleaning the room. He always followed her with his eyes, which repulsed her. He made excuses to be near her. His foul breath made her stomach churn.

She spent most of her days out of the house, helping the few wives in the fort with their sewing and mending. Only in the afternoon, when she knew Dirk had returned to the barracks, did she dare venture home.

"Good morning, Kitten. I wanted to tell you that I have to leave for a few days."

"What! Where are you going?" Glorianna tried to keep the rising note of panic from her voice as she noted the satisfied sneer that crossed Dirk's face.

"I have to go to Fort Lowell in Tucson on an inspection tour." Her father gently patted her cheek. "I'll be gone less than two weeks and I've asked Lieutenant Sullivan to keep an eye on you. Show him a little more respect and don't try so hard to avoid him." He frowned down at her. Glorianna lowered her eyes, willing away the tears.

"I'll be okay," she said. She looked up at her father. "Why can't you ask Timothy and Fayth Holwell to look after me? They live right next door, and I know they wouldn't mind."

Richard Wilton smiled at her. "I have asked them to help keep an eye on you, but I think it's possible you'll need more than Fayth and Timothy."

❧

"Oh, Fayth," Glorianna moaned, tugging at her sweat-soaked dress and fanning her hot face. "I don't know how anyone can live through this heat. Sometimes I think I'd be better able to bear it if I could wear my nightgown all the time."

"Why, that's it, Glorianna," Fayth said as a smile lit up her face.

"That's what?"

"The reason I bear the heat better than you do." Fayth informed her. "I still have to wear the dresses I used before I birthed Alyce."

Glorianna shook her head and grinned at her friend's enthusiasm. "I don't think I understand."

Fayth's voice took on the same tone as when she explained something to her young daughter. "My dresses are loose and yours are tight. Also, mine are lightweight calico and yours are heavier. Why don't we go over to Mr. Smith's store? I think he has some calico cloth. We can make you some dresses that will give you room to breathe and allow the air to flow through."

"What a wonderful idea, Fayth. Let's go right now."

By early afternoon, they had the first dress cut out and the stitching begun. Glorianna had two more lengths of material ready to start on as soon as she completed this dress.

"How are you and Conlon getting along these days?"

Glorianna bit her lip, trying to make it look like her sewing needed all her concentration. She waited until her feelings were more in control, then answered casually, "He follows me everywhere, but I've let him know I'm still waiting for Kendrick."

"You aren't beginning to like him, are you?" Fayth's penetrating gaze rested softly on Glorianna.

"I. . .uh, he is nice, but I know God wants me to marry Kendrick. That's what I want. Ouch!" Glorianna stuck her pinpricked finger into her mouth.

Fayth lifted Alyce to her lap. "I think perhaps you're spending more time thinking of Conlon than Kendrick. Don't you think it's possible that God brought you out here for a reason? Maybe He didn't think Kendrick would be the right husband for you."

"Are you on Conlon's side now?" Glorianna began to fold the material with jerky movements. "You know I might not mind him so much if he would quit pushing. He sticks closer to me than my shadow."

Fayth laughed. "He is a little presumptuous. But, his heart is right and I believe he's quite taken with you. I've watched the way he looks at you. Don't be too hasty to be rid of him."

"I'll try to be patient with him." Glorianna stood. "Now, I have to get home. I'll take the dress with me and work on it a bit more when the afternoon heat lets up. Thank you for the help."

Fayth walked to the door with Glorianna. "After all the help you've given everyone, I'm glad to finally be of some service to you."

Glorianna waded through the waves of heat, feeling the air pressing in on her. Oh, to get these tight clothes off and lie down for awhile. Her lack of sleep, combined with the close needlework, made her drowsy.

The interior of the house, though quiet, was only slightly cooler than the outside. The doors and windows were open, ready to draw in even the slightest afternoon breeze. She crossed to her room and put away her sewing. Taking the pins out of her hair, she shook it free and began to unbutton her dress.

"Now that's what I like to see." Glorianna froze as Dirk's whiskey-slurred words oozed across the room. She jerked her dress closed and turned her back to him.

"Mr. Smith, you will leave now or I'll speak to my father. If you have something you need to say to me, I'll be out in a moment."

In the quiet that followed, she could hear his shuffling footsteps getting nearer not farther away. Her heart began to pound. Her trembling hands fumbled madly at the undone buttons of her dress.

"It's okay, Missy, you don't need to fix up those buttons. You can open the rest if you want." A waft of whiskey-laden, rotten-toothed breath made her gag.

"Get out of here, Mr. Smith. Get out now, before my father comes."

A low chuckle turned her blood to ice. "Well, now, isn't it too bad the captain's gone. I guess he won't be here to see, will he?" One of his hands grasped her by the arm, pulling her back against him, while the other hand covered her mouth. Glorianna's scream of terror welled up too late to escape.

As quickly as he grabbed her, he let go. A strangled yelp echoed in her ear. "Perhaps the captain won't be here to see you, Dirk, but I will."

Glorianna nearly cried with relief at the sound of Conlon's voice. She turned around to see Conlon, his eyes hard and angry, holding Dirk in a grip of iron. Dirk's feet fought to touch the floor and his eyes bulged almost out of their sockets as Conlon twisted his collar tighter.

"I'd like to beat you senseless." Conlon's cold voice drained what little color was left in the pockmarked face. "Get back to the barracks. I'll deal with you later."

Setting the shorter man back on his feet, Conlon watched with Glorianna as Dirk sidled out the door. "Don't even think of trying to get away," Conlon called after him.

As Dirk disappeared through the door, Glorianna began to shake. She bit her lip, trying to hold back the sobs that welled up within. Suddenly, she felt herself engulfed in Conlon's strong arms. Without thinking, she leaned against his muscular chest and began to sob. For a long time she cried and trembled. He spoke soothing words and held her tight. His hand smoothed her long hair.

After awhile Glorianna's tears stopped. She rested against Conlon, noticing for the first time how wonderful it felt to be held within his strong embrace. She could hear the steady beating of his heart and feel the coarseness of his uniform tunic on her cheek.

Remembering where they were, Glorianna pushed away from Conlon. Her cheeks warmed in embarrassment. "Thank you, Lieutenant Sullivan," she said. "I'd appreciate it if you didn't say anything about this to anyone."

"Why didn't you report Dirk?" Conlon frowned. "I assume he's been making inappropriate gestures for awhile."

"He's my father's servant. It wasn't my place to question. Besides, I thought Mr. Smith to be harmless. Now, please go."

A slow smile spread across Conlon's face, lighting up the room and making Glorianna's heart beat faster. "Do you want me to leave because you don't think I'm harmless?" He lifted a hand as if to touch her, then paused. "I'll go, but I'll tell your father. He can pick someone else to help around the house." His tone turned more serious. "Don't worry, we'll keep this quiet."

❧

"Josiah." Conlon tried to make himself heard over the banging of the blacksmith's hammer. Josiah looked up and grinned, then thrust the piece of metal into the water to cool.

"Afternoon, Conlon. What are you doing out in this heat?"

"I guess I could ask the same of you. You're not only out in it, you're making more."

Josiah laughed, a hearty chuckle from deep inside. "This weather only reminds me how much I'll enjoy heaven when it's my turn to go. I don't want to lose sight of that."

Conlon grinned. "I can't imagine your losing sight of the Lord."

"So, what are you doing? I have the feeling you didn't come by here just to talk."

Looking around the blacksmith stall, Conlon paused a moment, rubbing his chin in thought. "I need to ask something of you, Josiah, and I need it kept quiet."

"You know me, Conlon. I'll not say anything."

"I know." Conlon smiled at his friend. "I need a pair of shackles I can fasten to a wall."

Josiah's eyebrows shot up as he looked at Conlon. "Why would you need those?" Then he hastily added, "Not that it's any of my business. You're in charge here with the captain away."

Conlon gazed out over the deserted parade ground before turning to Josiah. "One of the men tried to take liberties with the captain's daughter. I want to lock him up until the captain returns."

Black eyes flashed in anger as Josiah strode into the hot stall. He rummaged around in a box and soon returned with a set of cuffs. "These should do the trick. You can fasten them to the wall through here. Just don't tell me who the dirty dog is, or I might make these unnecessary."

Conlon nodded and hefted the heavy shackles. "I'll post a guard, too, but I don't plan to tell why the soldier's confined. Thanks."

"Say, Josiah." Conlon turned back as his friend picked up the lump of metal from the pail of water. "Can I ask you something?"

"Now what words of wisdom can I give you?" Josiah gave a mock bow.

"I'm a little stumped," Conlon hesitated. "You see, it's about Glorianna. I've tried to be patient with her, but she's just not coming around."

Josiah grinned. "You've been patient with her? That might be something to see." He chuckled. "Just how have you been courting her?"

"I try to be there all the time." Conlon frowned in thought.

"I walk her to breakfast and dinner. I check on her during the day and stop in of an evening to talk."

"Maybe you're suffocating the poor girl," Josiah suggested. "Why don't you back off a little and see if she comes around. Remember how you win a horse's affection. Sometimes you have to ignore the animal, then before you know it, that horse is nudging you on the shoulder."

"Are you suggesting Miss Wilton is like a horse?" Conlon grinned at Josiah's look of discomfort. "Thanks, Josiah. I'd better go before you start asking me what size shoes you should make for her."

❧

"Glorianna, are you there?" Fayth stepped through the open doorway.

"In here, Fayth." Glorianna splashed more water on her face, trying to erase the tearstains and puffiness.

"Guess what?" Fayth's eyes sparkled. "Timothy had the greatest idea."

"What is it?" Glorianna couldn't help but smile at her friend's obvious excitement.

"You know how the soldiers have taken to sleeping outside on their cots?" Glorianna nodded and Fayth continued. "Well, Timothy thinks we should do the same. That way, when there's a breeze, it won't be so hot and stuffy and we'll be able to rest."

"What a great idea." Relief flooded through Glorianna at the thought of more sleep. "In the middle of the night the air cools off outdoors. I can't wait to try this."

For the next hour, they carried out cots and situated them under trees so they wouldn't be too hot to lie upon. "Here, Glorianna, let's put your cot under this paloverde tree. It should shade you from the morning sun a bit and provide you some privacy."

"Are you bringing out a cot for Alyce, too?"

"Yes," Fayth said. "And, Lord willing, she'll be quiet through the night. She's been tossing and turning as much as the rest of us."

After supper, Glorianna, Fayth, and Timothy sat outside and talked until dark. Glorianna found herself watching for Conlon. He always showed up this time of night. It irritated her that, although she wanted him to leave her alone, the first time he did, all she could think about was his absence.

Later, when all was quiet, Glorianna crept out to her cot, praying no one would notice her in the dark. As she lay on the cot with the light breeze caressing her, she remembered the feel of Conlon's strong arms surrounding her. *His embrace felt so good.* But she quickly pushed the thought away and struggled to think about Kendrick.

Slowly, her body gave in to the demands of the day and weariness made her eyes drift shut. "Ouch!" Glorianna spluttered as she sat up in bed wondering what happened. At her movement another pain shot up her leg and fire flared on her arm.

"Glorianna, what's wrong?" Fayth called.

"Owww!" Glorianna brushed wildly at her arms and legs. She hopped off the cot, grabbed the sheet, and shook it out. "Bugs, Fayth. There are bugs all over my bed." With that she made a dash for the house before a certain lieutenant came running. It wouldn't do to have him catch her in her nightclothes.

four

"Are you sick, Miss Wilton?" Conlon stared at her as he pulled out a chair and sat down. Glorianna, already seated at the Holwells' breakfast table, felt the warmth of a blush in her cheeks.

"No, Mr. Sullivan, I don't have the measles or any other dread disease. I'm perfectly healthy." Glorianna slowly and carefully unfolded the cloth napkin and arranged it in her lap. She hoped Conlon would drop the embarrassing subject.

Conlon reached across the table and grabbed one of her hands. She winced as he rubbed his thumb across the swollen, red bumps on the back of her hand. "So, what caused these?"

"That's none of your business." Glorianna tugged at her hand. She glanced toward the other room where Fayth and Timothy were getting Alyce dressed.

"I have to disagree." Conlon grinned at her, holding her hand tightly despite her attempts to free it. "Your father asked me to look after you. What will he think when he returns and finds you covered with spots while I know nothing about their cause?"

"He also asked Fayth and Timothy to watch over me. They know exactly what happened, so you needn't worry yourself over it." With a jerk that rocked her in her chair, Glorianna pulled her hand free.

❧

"Good morning, Conlon." He stood as Fayth walked into the room. Timothy followed carrying a still sleepy Alyce. "Have you seen the nasty bites on Glorianna's hands?"

Conlon widened his eyes in mock surprise. "Bites? Now, who would be biting such a sweet young lady?"

Glorianna's face looked like a thundercloud as Fayth rose

29

to the bait and began to tell of their humiliating trial the night before. "When the bugs began to bite Glorianna, we all came inside knowing we would be next. Timothy's idea to sleep outside was good, but now we have to figure out how to get rid of the insects."

Conlon could feel his chest tighten as he tried to hold back the laughter. Poor Glorianna, or maybe that should be poor bugs. The thought was too much and a deep chuckle broke loose. Soon everyone but Glorianna was laughing. Even little Alyce chortled happily, waving a spoon in the air as if directing their laughter.

"Well, I don't see what's so funny about being chewed up by bugs." The red spots in Glorianna's cheeks burned bright.

"I'm sorry." Conlon stifled his laughter. "I just thought of those poor bugs not knowing what they were getting into when they bit you." Taking a deep breath he calmed himself. "I have an idea, Timothy. What do you think about putting the legs of the cots in cans of water? Then, if we keep the cots out from under the trees, the crawling bugs won't get on them anyway."

"That sounds good." Timothy nodded. "I know Alyce is happy this morning, but she fussed all night because of the heat and the couple of ant bites she got. I don't want to go through that again."

Conlon ate quickly, noticing how often Glorianna rubbed at her hands. He knew how nasty those ant bites could be. Excusing himself, he followed Fayth into the kitchen. A few minutes later, he knelt beside Glorianna. Before she could object, he plucked her hand off her lap.

"Has God told you this is the time to ask me to marry you, Lieutenant? I'll tell you right now the answer is 'no.' "

Conlon grinned. "I hadn't thought of asking you quite yet, Miss Wilton. I'll be sure to let you know when it's time. Right now, I have something to help take the itch out of those bug bites." With that, he began to smear a white paste over the swollen bites.

"What are you putting on her?" Fayth moved around the table to watch. "Can I use it on Alyce?"

"It's just a mixture of baking soda and water. Doc Clark told me about it when I ran into a bunch of ants awhile back. If you put it on wet and let it dry it helps. If Alyce eats it, it won't hurt her. She probably won't like the taste, though."

Conlon handed the bowl of paste to Glorianna. "I'm sure you have other bites you would rather tend yourself." He smiled as pink stained her cheeks. He didn't want to let her know how hard it was to hold her hand in his and act like it didn't affect him. He remembered well the feel of holding her in his arms yesterday. He could still smell the faint scent of roses and feel the silkiness of her hair. *God, please help me to be patient,* he pleaded. *Help me find a common ground, something we both enjoy.*

"You know, Conlon," Fayth smiled sweetly at him, "Glorianna mentioned that she loves horses. Perhaps you could give her a quick tour of the stables."

"You like horses, too?" Conlon turned to Glorianna, astonished at the immediate answer to his prayer. "We have plenty of time before the nine o'clock guard-mount and roll calls begin. Would you like to see our horses?"

Glorianna, the bowl of paste gripped in her hands, looked like she couldn't decide whether to stay mad or succumb to her desire to visit the stables. "I'd love to see the horses," she said finally. "Do you think I could have a minute to finish putting on some of this paste?" She grimaced. "I know I'll be more comfortable."

❧

"This is my horse, Champ." Conlon's pride in the beautiful buckskin couldn't be hidden.

Glorianna slipped her hand over the stall door. Champ gently nudged her, his soft muzzle tickling her palm. "He's beautiful. Is he your own, or does he belong to the cavalry?"

"He's mine." Conlon reached up to tug on the horse's black forelock. "I brought him with me when I came out here from Kentucky. Come on, I'll show you the other horses Fayth's favorite is right down here. She enjoys riding when someone has the time to go with her."

"Why does someone have to go with her?"

Conlon frowned. "Out here, there's danger everywhere. Between the Indians, rattlers, and cougars, it's best not to go out alone. And, in these wide-open spaces you can get lost pretty quickly. You need to remember that."

Glorianna followed Conlon down the aisle of stalls. "I couldn't see any danger when we came across the desert from Yuma. We didn't see a single rattlesnake. I don't think there's much to worry about."

"Glorianna, as long as I'm in charge of your safety, I want you to promise me you'll always have someone with you when you go riding." Conlon paused, his stern expression firming Glorianna's resolve to ride by herself as soon as she had the chance. "If I can't accompany you, then one of the other men will. Promise?"

"Oh, all right. I suppose I have to or you'll give orders that I can't have a horse to ride." *But, as soon as my father returns and you aren't in charge of my welfare, we'll see what happens.*

"Good." Conlon's grin set her heart pounding. "Now, let's see which horse you take a liking to."

"Oh, this one." Glorianna peered over the stall at a beautiful sorrel with a flaxen mane and tail. His head arched proudly, and his white socks flashed as he turned and pranced toward her.

"I must say you have excellent taste in horses, but I'm afraid this one is off limits, even to the captain's daughter."

"And why is that?"

"Because this is a man's horse, Miss Wilton. He's too high-spirited for a lady. We'll find you something a little calmer."

Conlon started off down the row of stalls. Glorianna stood by the sorrel's stall, hands clenched at her sides, waiting for Conlon to realize she wasn't following.

"Aren't you coming?" Conlon turned back to face her.

"Lieutenant Sullivan, I have always ridden spirited horses. I can easily control this horse, and you haven't given me a single reason why I shouldn't be allowed to ride him. You'll have to come up with something better than his being a man's horse."

Conlon slowly traced his steps back to her side, the soft dirt of the stable floor silencing his footsteps. He stopped in front of her, his blue eyes twinkling as if he was laughing at her. "Miss Wilton, this horse belongs to Josiah Washington, our blacksmith. To my knowledge no one else even feeds the horse, let alone rides him. Now, if you want to take on Josiah, you may do so, but I'll warn you he's quite a bit stronger than you."

Glorianna tried to step back, wanting to distance herself from Conlon. The stable wall stopped her. Why did his nearness always affect her this way? Rather than pursuing her desire to ride this horse, she found herself wanting to look at Conlon. She wanted to watch the way his blue eyes sparkled with humor. To brush that stray lock of hair off his forehead. To touch his handsome, chiseled face.

With a mental shake, Glorianna brought herself around. "I will talk with Mr. Washington at the first available moment, Lieutenant. Right now, I believe it's time to return home."

Conlon stepped back, bowed low, sweeping his arm toward the door. "Allow me to escort you, Miss Wilton."

Glorianna lifted her chin and swept past him, heading down the passage between the stalls. She studiously ignored the arm Conlon offered her. "I can find my own way back, Lieutenant. I'm sure you have other matters to attend. The morning inspection is fast approaching."

A sudden influx of soldiers proved Glorianna's point. Loud, raucous laughter filled the stables as the troops headed for their tack and horses to get ready for the drills and calls. She halted, unsure how to proceed with so many men in the way. The firm pressure of Conlon's hand on her elbow was a welcome relief, although she determined he would never know it.

"I'll get you to where the ladies will be gathering. Then I'm afraid I'll have to get Champ ready." Conlon's soft words spoken close to her ear sent a shiver down her spine.

❧

Although her parasol blocked the sun's rays, it did little to cool the rising heat of the morning. Despite the warmth, Glorianna stared at the parade of horses and men, captivated with the beauty and symmetry of their movements. The proud horses' bowed necks complemented their riders' straight backs and oneness with their mounts.

"There's Timothy." Fayth's pride in her husband shone on her face. Glorianna glanced at her, then followed the direction she looked and managed to spot Timothy Holwell riding a bay. The horse's dark brown coat gleamed in the sun.

"I still have some trouble knowing who's who," Glorianna admitted. "When they're in uniform and have their caps on, they all look alike." She sent an apologetic smile in Fayth's direction.

Fayth laughed and bounced Alyce higher on her hip. "Don't worry, we've all been through that. Imagine how I felt when I couldn't even recognize my own husband. You'll do better in no time."

Glorianna didn't know how she would ever tell one soldier from another. Even the horses were starting to blend together.

"Look, there's Conlon riding out on Champ."

Glorianna looked across the parade ground. Conlon's shining buckskin pranced to the center of the parade ground. His black-socked legs pistoned up and down in precision movements. Champ's black mane and tail perfectly complemented his gleaming tan hide. Conlon sat ramrod stiff, every inch the cavalry officer. The stable call began, each rider rigid in the saddle as he paraded in front of his commanding officer.

As they rode past, Glorianna found herself comparing each rider to Conlon. Every man in the cavalry lacked something. He was either too short, too slouchy, or too thin; not one of them could compare in looks.

"Didn't you love the call-to-arms?" Fayth whispered as the last of the horses high-stepped past. "I've seen it more times than I can count, and I still get a thrill from it."

"I don't know which I liked best," Glorianna admitted as they ambled toward their houses. Each of them held one of Alyce's small hands as she toddled between them. "Watching the soldiers leap for their rifles and the officers buckle on their swords in the call-to-arms could take your breath away. Then again, the sight of all those mounted soldiers sitting so perfectly on their glistening horses reminded me of knights in shining armor. I couldn't help but wonder what it would be like to be swept off my feet and ride off into the sunset with one of them."

Fayth stopped and stared open-mouthed at Glorianna. "Are you telling me you're falling for Lieutenant Sullivan? I just knew you wouldn't be able to resist him."

"I did not say I was falling for anyone." Glorianna felt a blush heat her cheeks. "Remember Kendrick? He would make a wonderful knight in shining armor. Perhaps I'll go write a letter and tell him. Maybe I need to let him know exactly what my feelings are."

Quickly, Glorianna left her new friend and rushed across the parade ground toward her quarters. She tried to forget the small lie she'd told Fayth about picturing Kendrick as a knight. Instead, she began to plan how to word a letter to him. But, for some reason, she couldn't shut out the image of all those cavalrymen and horses. The vibrant picture of Conlon Sullivan sitting so straight and tall left little room to remember a passing acquaintance she hadn't seen for months.

❧

As darkness fell, Glorianna, wrapped in a light blanket, made her way to the cot prepared for her. She sank down exhausted from so many nights of fitful sleep. As the cool night breeze washed over her, she drifted into a night of peaceful, much-needed sleep. She didn't even consider whether the cans of water would do their work, she simply slept.

five

Towering maple and oak trees shaded them as Glorianna and her cousin, Kathleen O'Connor, strolled down the street. The quiet afternoon muted their conversation. Carriages rolled soundlessly down the rain-washed street. Other than the faint buzz of bees busy about their work, they were the only two in this world of silence.

Glorianna stopped, placing a restraining hand on her cousin's arm. "Look, Kathleen, it's him."

Kathleen turned her freckled pixie face toward Glorianna. "Who?" she asked, her hazel eyes darkening in question.

"It's Kendrick. Can't you see him?"

Glorianna watched as Kathleen shook her head, her mahogany curls swinging with the motion. "I don't want to see him, Glory. I don't want you to see him, either. I've told you before he isn't worth your time."

"But, he's so handsome. I know you don't think he's a Christian, but he goes to church."

"Oh, Glory." Kathleen frowned at her. "You know the only time he attends church is when he can get a free meal or some entertainment. Besides, a man who loved God wouldn't get himself into as many scrapes as Kendrick does."

"He leads an interesting life." Glorianna twirled the handle of her parasol. "It would be so exciting to be married to him. Think of all the adventures you would have."

"I refuse to think of them," Kathleen said. "I wouldn't even allow him to call on me. If you know what's good for you, you'll discourage him, too."

"But, God wants me to marry Kendrick. I'm sure of it."

"How do you know such a thing, Glory? Doesn't the Bible say we shouldn't be unequally yoked? Have you stopped to *look at Kendrick through God's eyes?"*

"And what would God look for that I haven't?"

"I believe God would look for a man that will pray and read the Bible regularly with his family. Will Kendrick do that?" Kathleen's honest assessment made Glorianna fidget. *"God wants a man for you who will take you to church every week. Will Kendrick do that?"*

"He will." Glorianna tipped her parasol to the side so she could get a better look at her cousin. She hoped her doubts weren't reflected in her eyes. *"He just needs some encouragement. He hasn't come from a Christian home. That makes it hard for him. A good wife will bring out the best in him."*

"Glorianna." She turned as the deep voice called her name. Kendrick stood there, his face set in its customary haughty smile. The persistent buzzing of bees near her head grew louder, but she ignored it. As she watched, his pale blue eyes deepened to a morning glory blue and filled with kindness. His blond hair darkened to black and his haughty expression changed to one of love. But he wasn't Kendrick anymore. What was happening?

"Don't move," he warned. "Please stay still."

She looked in confusion to see him raising a gun. Before she could even cry out, smoke belched from the gun's barrel and a loud bang reverberated through the air. Glorianna screamed and leapt from her cot.

"It's okay, Sweetheart." Suddenly, Conlon's arms were around her. Once again, she found herself sobbing into his shoulder, completely disoriented.

"I'm sorry, I thought you were awake. I didn't mean to scare you."

Glorianna pushed herself back from him. "You shot at me." Fear made her want to scream at him. "And I am not your sweetheart!"

"Glorianna, look." Conlon grabbed her by the shoulders and turned her around. There, on the ground beneath her cot, a headless rattlesnake writhed in its death throes. Glorianna's knees buckled. If he hadn't been behind her, she would have collapsed on the ground.

"I tried to warn you to lie still. I didn't want you to get off your cot with the snake under there." The sound of running footsteps startled her and Glorianna realized she had nothing on but her nightdress.

"Oh!" She grabbed for her thin blanket, still crumpled on the cot. Running for her house, she could feel the heat of embarrassment burning her cheeks. What had Conlon been doing by her cot anyway? Did he spy on her while she slept? Maybe it wasn't worth the comfort of sleeping outside if it tempted him to watch her. She would question him about this later.

꙳

"Hello?" Fayth's light knock and query echoed through the silent house. Glorianna's trembling fingers fumbled at the final button of her dress.

"I'll be out in a moment." Glorianna hated the shreds of fear in her voice. She could still hear the buzzing from her dream and see the twitching body of the snake. The buzz hadn't been from bees as she dreamed. If she had gotten off her cot, the snake would have bitten her in an instant, before she was fully awake. She shuddered and took a deep breath to calm her queasy stomach.

"Are you okay?" Fayth's concern showed in the paleness of her face.

Glorianna forced a tentative smile. "I'm fine, I think. I'm just a little shaky. It isn't every morning I wake up to such excitement."

Fayth hugged her tight. "Timothy and I were so scared when we heard the shot. Thank God, Conlon happened along when he did."

"That's something that has me a little upset, too." Glorianna stiffened at the reminder of Conlon's seeing her in her nightdress. "What was he doing by my bed?"

Fayth smiled and grabbed Glorianna's hands, holding them tight. "I believe God sent him. You see, we invited him for breakfast again. For some reason, you slept late. When he rounded the corner and saw you still asleep, he planned to walk on by."

"Then why didn't he?" Glorianna tried hard to hold on to her anger.

"Why? Because he heard the rattler. He couldn't very well leave you defenseless, could he?"

"I suppose not." A chill raced through her, raising bumps on her arms. "I don't know why I slept so late, anyway. I never do."

"But, don't you see?" Fayth continued, the excitement in her voice demanding Glorianna's attention. "God planned that. If you had awakened earlier, no one would have been there to kill the snake. It might have struck at you."

"I could have died."

"Yes, that's possible, but sometimes a person only gets sick from rattlesnake bites. If the venom gets drawn out right away, there's a good chance they will live."

Glorianna nodded, hoping she would never need to recall that information. She didn't ever want to see another snake again, especially one with rattles on its tail.

"Now, how about coming to our house for some breakfast? You look a little pale and I'm sure you're hungry. Emily should have the food ready to set on the table."

"I'd love to. Let me run a brush through my hair first. I don't want to scare Alyce." She attempted a smile, not sure her stomach would welcome any food. Still, she didn't want to upset Fayth, who was so thoughtfully trying to help.

❧

Heat from the blacksmith's forge washed over Glorianna in waves, overwhelming the warmth of even the desert sun. Sweat beaded on her brow and threatened to trickle down her face. She sopped it with her handkerchief and pulled her parasol forward to block the hotter waves which radiated in front of her.

The smell of burning wood and the steady bang of the

hammer against the anvil shut out the world around her. Mesmerized, Glorianna watched the blacksmith rhythmically pound a piece of red-hot metal, molding it into the u-shape of a horseshoe.

She hadn't seen the blacksmith before. If he was standing straight and not bent over his forge, he would tower over her. His muscles rippled and bulged, sweat covering his bare, ebony arms in a mirrored sheen. His huge hands looked as though one of them would wrap quite easily around her neck. A tremor of fear swept through her. Was this what Conlon meant about being brave enough to ask about riding the blacksmith's horse? Would this giant take offense and swat her away like a bothersome fly? Trepidation shivered down her spine. She stepped back. Maybe it would be best to slip away before he noticed her.

But the thought came to her too late. The blacksmith turned and thrust the heated metal into a pail of water. Steam hissed and rose in a cloud around him. His inky gaze locked on her, and a slow grin split his face.

"Good evening." His booming voice held her fast. "You must be the captain's daughter."

"I–I am." Glorianna swallowed hard, trying to regain her composure and remember why she was here.

"I'm Josiah Washington." The massive head dipped toward her. "I'm pleased to meet you."

Hot air swirled around Glorianna. She felt lightheaded. She gritted her teeth, determined not to faint simply because this man looked like the makings of a nightmare. He sounded friendly enough, and his smile, although crooked, appeared pleasant.

Glorianna forced herself to meet Josiah's jet black gaze. Suddenly, she knew with certainty that this man would never hurt anyone. His eyes were gentle and innocent. She smiled, then relaxed for the first time since approaching the blacksmith's forge.

"I'm sorry to bother you, Mr. Washington. You're right,

I'm the captain's daughter, Glorianna. I'd like to ask a favor of you."

"And what might that be?"

"Yesterday, Lieutenant Sullivan took me on a tour of the stables. I happen to love horses. I learned to ride almost before I could walk. When I saw your horse, I wanted to ride him. Lieutenant Sullivan said you wouldn't allow me, but I should ask you myself."

Josiah picked up a rag and swabbed the rivers of sweat off his face. He looked at her, the smile wiped from his face as well. "I don't let anyone ride Sultan, Miss Wilton. I'm sorry to disappoint you, but he's a bit picky about who rides him."

"I'm used to handling difficult horses." Glorianna heard her voice rising, hating the sound of it. "Perhaps, if you give me a chance."

"I would gladly share anything I have with you, Miss Wilton." Josiah held her with his steady gaze. "But the truth is, I know that horse. He isn't just difficult; he can get mean. His former owner didn't treat him so good. I've seen him throw a man and then turn to pound him into the ground. I'd never forgive myself if something like that happened to you."

Glorianna stood silent, watching the gentle giant. Now she understood why no one but Josiah even fed the horse. For some reason, the horse trusted him. He might not feel that way about her or anyone else. Josiah wasn't denying her out of selfishness; he wanted to protect her.

"Thank you, Mr. Washington, I understand."

Before she could turn to go, Josiah spoke again. "There are plenty of good horses in that stable, Miss Wilton. I'm sure the lieutenant will be happy to pick one out for you."

❧

Heavy footsteps thundered across the front room. Glorianna looked up from where she sat cross-legged on her bed writing a letter to Kathleen. A thread of fear wove its way through her. "Who's there?"

"Kitten, it's me." Glorianna cried out at the sound of her

father's deep, rumbling voice. Tossing aside her pen and paper, she hopped off the bed and ran to him. Her father wrapped his arms around her, holding her tight.

"I'm so sorry," he murmured. "I had no idea Dirk would try such a thing."

"It's not your fault, Daddy." Glorianna smiled up at him through her tears. "Everything turned out fine, thanks to Lieutenant Sullivan."

"I hear he's been taking good care of you." Her father grinned down at her. "I've heard stories of his fighting snakes of all kinds."

Glorianna could feel the heat of a blush on her cheeks. She pushed back from her father, not wanting to admit how grateful she was for Conlon's protection. "He only did his job." She sounded petty, even to her own ears.

"I'd say he went beyond duty." Her father's reprimand made her feel like a child. His quick smile eased her discomfort. "I do want to say that I've released Dirk. He says it was only the liquor. He won't be around you, though." Her father hugged her again. "Now, enough about that. I've brought a couple of things for you from Tucson. Come with me."

Glorianna followed her father into the kitchen. A young girl turned from the cupboards to face them. Her dark hair and eyes blended with her olive complexion. She looked down and shuffled her bare feet on the floor.

"This is Maria. Maria, this is my daughter, Glorianna." He turned back to Glorianna. "Maria will cook for us and keep the house. If you need anything, just ask. She speaks quite a bit of English."

"Hello, Maria." Glorianna smiled at the pretty Mexican girl. "Thank you for coming to help us out."

Maria nodded quickly and smiled. "Happy to, *Señorita*. Make good food for you."

Slipping her hand onto her father's proffered arm, Glorianna allowed herself to be escorted out of the kitchen. Her father grinned at her. "Now, I have something outside for you."

Glorianna stared in amazement as she stepped into the muted evening sun. Conlon Sullivan stood in the shade of a paloverde tree holding the reins of a beautiful horse. Her sorrel coat and flaxen mane and tail reminded Glorianna of Josiah Washington's Sultan. Four white socks colored her trim legs and a slender white strip ran down her nose. Small ears perked forward as Glorianna and her father approached.

"I know how much you like horses, Kitten. This spunky little mare needed a good home, and I thought of you."

"She's mine?" Glorianna gasped. "Oh, she's so beautiful." She gently stroked the soft neck. She looked across the mare at Conlon and smiled as the horse leaned her head over and rubbed her ear against his arm.

"She seems to like you, Lieutenant." Glorianna turned to her father. "What's her name?" Excitement made her chatter like Alyce.

"She doesn't have one." Her father shook his head. "I guess you'll have to think of a suitable name for her."

"Oh, I don't know." Glorianna paused as she stroked the soft muzzle. "She's such a sweet little girl. Do you have any ideas, Lieutenant?"

"I'd say you just named her." Conlon grinned, his blue eyes sparkling. "Little girl in Spanish is *nina*. That sounds like a good name."

"*Nina*," Glorianna whispered. "I like it. When can I ride her?" She swung around toward her father.

"You may go now if Lieutenant Sullivan will accompany you."

Glorianna turned back to Conlon. She wanted so much to ride Nina, even if it meant going with Conlon Sullivan.

He chuckled in obvious delight with the prospect. "I'm ready to go. Champ is saddled at the stables. I'll get him while you change into your riding habit."

Scampering inside, Glorianna couldn't contain her excitement. *I'll just pretend I'm riding with Kendrick,* she concluded, not at all sure she would manage the pretense.

six

Nina's smooth, rocking gait thrilled Glorianna. Her father had given her the perfect gift. She missed the riding she had done in the East. On the days her mother didn't need her so much, she always took the opportunity to go for a refreshing ride. Nothing equaled the feeling of freedom that came from sitting on a spirited horse.

"Where shall we go, Lieutenant?"

Conlon took a long look around them, as if trying to decide the best direction. "It occurred to me that you haven't seen much of our desert. You probably have no idea that we have a river near the camp."

"A river? Here?" Glorianna couldn't mask her astonishment.

"That's right." Conlon laughed aloud. "Would you like to ride down to the Verde with me?"

"I'd love to." Glorianna followed Conlon down a wide trail. Memories assaulted her, the freshest one also the most painful. . .

❧

"Glorianna." Her mother's weak voice barely reached her.

"What is it?" she asked, hurrying to take her mother's thin, dry hand in her own. "What do you need?"

"Please ride to the river. See if you can find some spring flowers and bring me a few." Her mother collapsed back into the pillow, weakened by the speech. "I want to see their beauty one more time." Glorianna leaned close to hear the words.

Glorianna galloped to the river as fast as she dared over the uneven ground. Was her mother dying? Dr. Prince told her only yesterday that it wouldn't be long. She wasn't ready though. She would never be ready. Tears streamed down her face, the whipping wind drying them as they fell.

At the river, Glorianna slipped off her horse near a patch of bluebells, her mother's favorite. As she bent to pick a bouquet of the delicate flowers, a tinkle of laughter caught her attention. Her horse's reins in one hand, flowers in the other, she rounded the bend of the river.

Seated on the riverbank were three girls and a group of five boys. The boys were all friends of Kendrick's. The girls all attended the same church as Glorianna and her mother. Glorianna took another step closer and noticed a couple seated on the ground, partially hidden by a huge oak tree.

Kendrick and Melissa Cornwall—syrupy, beautiful, wealthy Melissa Cornwall—were engaged in intimate conversation. He leaned back against the tree and she rested her hand on his chest, batting her blue eyes at him. Glorianna wanted to scream. How could he look at her like that?

Glorianna backed out of sight and swung back on her horse. On the way home, the tears weren't for her mother, they were for her and her inability to fight for the man she wanted to marry.

At home she put away her horse, wiped her eyes, and headed toward the house. "You won't get away with this, Melissa," she whispered. "Kendrick is mine and I'll not let you have him."

She put the small bouquet of flowers in a vase and took it to her mother's room. Her mother was no longer there. Only her body remained, an empty shell. Her spirit had gone home to be with the Lord.

Within a few days, Glorianna was heading west to be with her father. She had no chance to fight for Kendrick.

She had to get back before it was too late and Melissa won.

≈

"Miss Wilton?" Conlon called for the third time. He reined Champ closer and touched her hand where it rested on the saddle. She started, and her green eyes focused on him for the first time in several minutes. "Are you okay?"

A slight shudder shook her slender frame and Glorianna said, "I'm fine, Lieutenant. I apologize for my lack of manners. I was just remembering my last ride before I came west."

"Do you want to talk about it?" Conlon studied her pale face. "You looked so sad."

Glorianna shrugged, a sad, faraway look on her face. "I rode to a river near us to bring some flowers for my mother." She paused, then continued in a near whisper. "She died before I returned."

"I'm sorry," Conlon said, reaching over to squeeze her small hand lightly. She didn't pull back, and he clasped her cool fingers for a moment to warm them.

Glorianna attempted a smile. "I know she's happier with the Lord. It's just that I miss her so."

As if she realized her vulnerability, Glorianna pulled her hand from his. "Maybe this isn't the best time to ride to the river. I'd like to go back home, please."

Conlon nodded and let Champ follow Nina as Glorianna reined her around in the road. *Why does she seem so open, then suddenly close up on me? Just when I think we're starting to become friends, she puts up a wall and shuts me out.* He stroked Champ's sweaty neck and watched Glorianna's fingers whiten on her reins. *Something is bothering her,* he thought. *Lord, help me learn how I can reach her and help her through this difficult time. I know she misses her mother, but it's more than that, I think.*

ʖ

"Glorianna! Conlon!" Fayth waved wildly from her seat in the ambulance. The boxlike wagon was often used to transport cavalry wives and children to various destinations. "Come with us," Fayth said as Conlon and Glorianna drew near. "We're going to the Verde River to bathe and cool off." Beyond the wagon a group of cavalrymen sat astride their horses.

Conlon looked at Glorianna and shrugged, giving her the opportunity to answer. "I don't know, Fayth." Glorianna tried to smile. "I don't have any other clothes with me."

"I took care of that." Fayth held up a wrapped bundle. "I was hoping we'd run into you, so I brought some extra things. Come on," she pleaded. "Alyce will love having you along, and it will feel wonderful to be cool for a few minutes." Alyce clapped her hands as if agreeing with her mother.

"All right." Glorianna laughed at the toddler's antics. "I guess we'll just ride behind you."

"If you would like, Miss Wilton, I'll take Nina back to the camp. You can ride in the ambulance with the others."

"Aren't you coming, Conlon?" Fayth frowned at him.

"I want to get some clean clothes. I'll catch up with you," Conlon said. "Don't worry, I won't miss out on a chance to cool off."

Conlon dismounted and helped Glorianna into the wagon. She settled onto the seat next to Fayth. Alyce climbed over to snuggle into her lap and Glorianna hugged the tiny girl, drawing comfort from her.

The ambulance jolted into motion, nearly unseating several of the women. They laughed and chattered with one another. Glorianna tried to ignore the emptiness gnawing a hole inside her.

"Has anyone told you about the cactus here?" Fayth leaned close to be heard over the other women's chatter.

Glorianna looked at all the strange plants by the side of the road and shook her head. "I don't know much about them. I wouldn't know what to avoid and what's safe."

"Just in case you're ever watching Alyce, let me explain which ones she shouldn't play near." Fayth grinned. "The last thing I want is a daughter that comes in looking like she's been in a fight with a porcupine." They both laughed. For the remainder of the ride to the river, Fayth pointed out various plants and explained their dangers or purposes.

Before long, they arrived at the Verde River. Having caught up with them, Conlon joined the men tromping along the path leading farther down the river. The women slipped and slid down the nearest trail to the cool water.

"Hey, stop that," Glorianna laughed as Alyce splashed water in her face. Alyce chuckled and did it again. "I'll get you wet if you don't stop," Glorianna warned. Alyce squealed and slammed both hands down on the water, shooting a spray into Glorianna's face.

"Alyce, you behave." Fayth's lips pursed as if she held back a smile.

"Don't worry. We're just having a little fun." Glorianna splashed water on Alyce's stomach. They laughed, enjoying the cool river water.

Later, as Fayth, Alyce, and Glorianna relaxed in the shallow water, Fayth asked, "Are you upset about Dirk being released?"

Glorianna shrugged and watched Alyce pick up rocks from the river bottom. "He said he only did it because he was drunk. I'll just stay away from him." She picked up a handful of rocks, then dribbled them back into the river. "I guess I am a little nervous."

Alyce's head nodded forward. Fayth chuckled as she picked her daughter up. "I think you're about to fall asleep in the water." She stood and began to wade toward the bank.

"I'll go up to the wagon and fetch our clothes," Glorianna called. "I'll only be a minute."

Following the faint path up from the river to the road, the sounds of women's laughter faded away. The quiet peacefulness of the desert settled around Glorianna. She hoped none of the men were at the wagon yet. She didn't like the idea of them seeing her in wet clothing, particularly a certain lieutenant who had the bad habit of catching her off guard.

Glorianna peered into the wagon searching through the bundles of clothing for the one Fayth wrapped up for them. She lifted the bulky garments and turned back to the trail down to the river. Hands grabbed her arms. Before she could react she was crushed against a wet body.

"Well, well, looky who we have here." Dirk's fetid breath

didn't smell of alcohol this time. Glorianna's heart almost stopped, then beat a frantic rhythm as she struggled to free herself from his iron grip.

"Let me go, now," she hissed. "You won't have the excuse of being drunk this time. You know what my father will do."

He laughed. Glorianna turned her head, trying to avoid his foul breath and the unsightly glimpse of rotted teeth. She pushed against his chest, hitting him with her fists.

"That's what I like, sweet thing. A woman with spirit. You and I will get along fine." He laughed and tried to pull her closer. "You just need a little time to get used to the idea of us together."

"Leave me alone." Glorianna's body was taut with fear. "If you don't let go, I'll scream. You know that help isn't far."

A hand clamped over her mouth before she could say more. "Then I guess I'll just have to keep you quiet." His sinister laugh sent a chill coursing down her spine. "No one will hear you now. They're all having too much fun in the river."

Glorianna strained against Dirk as he tried to pull her tighter against him. She wanted to bite his hand and loosen his grip just long enough to get out a scream, but he pushed it painfully tight over her mouth. She relaxed, hoping he would think she was giving in and let down his guard for a minute.

"That's right, sweet thing." Dirk leaned closer to her. "I knew you'd understand. No one will help you this time."

"No one, Dirk? I think you're wrong there," Conlon's voice held a deadly calm.

Dirk whirled, releasing Glorianna. She fell to the ground. He crouched low. A knife appeared in his hand as if by magic. Without thinking, Glorianna swept her feet forward, knocking them into Dirk's legs. He lost his balance and stumbled forward.

Like a streak of lightning, Conlon's fist caught Dirk on the jaw, knocking him backward. With his other hand, Conlon grabbed Dirk's arm and banged it against the wagon. The knife clattered to the ground.

Glorianna scooted backward, trying her best to put some distance between herself and the fighters. She winced as Conlon picked Dirk up from the dirt and hit him again. Blood from Dirk's nose streamed down the front of his shirt. Conlon's eyes were dark with anger. He pummeled Dirk, knocking him back against the ambulance.

"I warned you once," Conlon snarled. "I told you to stay away from Glorianna."

Dirk dodged Conlon and wiped his nose with his sleeve. "You just want her for yourself, Lieutenant. You figure you're the Cap'n's pet so you should get her. Well, you aren't the only one in the game."

Conlon let out a low growl and lunged for Dirk. Glorianna screamed. Yells and the pounding of heavy footsteps sounded in the brush. A moment later, Timothy Holwell and several of the other men appeared from the river path. Timothy grabbed Conlon while the other men restrained Dirk.

"Tie him up," Conlon ordered. "We'll take him back to the camp and let the captain handle this."

Timothy loosened his hold and Conlon walked over to Glorianna. He slipped a hand under her elbow and helped her over to the wagon. "Are you okay?" he asked, concern evident in his voice.

"I'll be fine." Glorianna tried to keep her voice steady. She wanted Conlon to take her in his arms and comfort her, but knew he wouldn't with all the men around. The excited voices of the women were coming closer as they climbed the path from the river. "Thank you for rescuing me again, Lieutenant. You seem to do it very well."

Conlon grinned down at her, his eyes a deep warm blue again. "It's truly my pleasure."

❧

Conlon lay on his cot watching the panorama of celestial splendor overhead. But a mental image of a beautiful redhead with vivid green eyes overshadowed the stars. She seemed so sad today when they were riding. He longed to hold her and comfort her.

His hands clenched as he remembered finding Glorianna once more in the clutches of Dirk. Never had he felt such rage. The thought of that lowlife touching Glorianna filled him with fresh anger. At least it wouldn't happen again. The captain had agreed to lock Dirk up until they could ship him to Fort Lowell in Tucson. Conlon wanted to hang him.

God, I'm sorry I'm having such a hard time with forgiveness here. Please help me. Teach me how to reach out to Glorianna without being pushy. I'm so used to getting what I want that I'm having trouble waiting for You, Lord. I want to learn patience. I know I'll need it throughout life, and I may as well start right now.

Conlon drifted off to sleep, a smile relaxing his face. Memories of sweet rose scent and silken fiery red hair filled his thoughts and dreams.

seven

"Looks like rain might finally be a possibility." Fayth pointed at the sky as she and Glorianna left the mercantile.

Over the desert, billowing clouds played hide and seek with the sun. The wind whipped the women's dresses against their legs. The blowing sand stung as it tried to imbed itself in their tender skin. Fayth handed her package to Glorianna and sheltered Alyce's face against her neck.

"The summer storms are late this year." Fayth led the way across the deserted parade ground. "Usually, we've had some rain by now and the dust isn't so bad as this."

"What exactly are they?" Glorianna squinted against the wind. "Isn't one storm like another?"

Fayth shook her head and leaned farther over Alyce. "These are more than normal storms. They bring lightning, strong winds, and, we hope, rain. The temperature drops drastically. Sometimes, we don't get the rain. Then the lightning starts fires in the dry brush of the desert. The early ones are always a little scary because the desert is so dry. Of course, it's possible these clouds won't amount to anything."

Fayth opened the door to her house. Glorianna stepped in and started to close the door when a shout stopped her. She turned to see Conlon striding toward her; his eyes fastened on her, disregarding the strong breeze. Her heartbeat quickened and she tried to ignore how much she looked forward to seeing him.

Conlon waved something at her, his mouth moving, but the words were ripped away by the wind. He strode closer, then called again, "I have a letter for you."

Fayth returned to take the packages. Glorianna tried to remain calm as Conlon approached. She didn't know whether her excitement stemmed from seeing him or from getting a letter. Oh, it would be good to hear from home.

"It looks like you heard from someone back east."

Standing in the doorway with Conlon on the steps below her, they were almost the same height. She had no trouble gazing into his sparkling blue eyes. In fact, she had trouble looking away. Mesmerized, she watched the wind play games with his dark hair, flinging it on his forehead, then sweeping it back over his brow.

"Your mail, Miss Wilton."

Glorianna started, then felt the heat of a blush rising. She'd been staring at Conlon like a sentimental schoolgirl. He held out her letter, grinning as if he knew her every thought.

"Thank you, Lieutenant," she stammered. Struggling to regain control, she stared at the envelope, then called to Fayth, "I've gotten a letter from my cousin Kathleen. I'm going to run home and read it." She brushed past Conlon, trying to ignore the feelings he caused, trying to forget the impish grin that set her heart pounding.

Clasping the precious missive to her chest so it wouldn't blow away, Glorianna hurried to get inside. She closed the door and ripped open the envelope.

Glory,

I thought I should tell you about Kendrick. I know you had your heart set on the scoundrel, though I can't understand why. Half the girls around here feel the same way you do. I'm glad he never overwhelmed me.

But, enough with the lecture. I'm sorry to carry on like that. I wanted to write and let you know that Kendrick and Melissa Cornwall have announced their engagement. They are planning a November wedding. I know you can't be here for it and probably wouldn't want to anyway. I'm sorry to be the bearer of bad news. You should get on with your life. I've heard there are plenty of men in the West and not many women. I'm sure

*you can find a godly husband, once you forget about
Kendrick.*

Glorianna set the rest of the letter down on the bed. Tears
blurred her vision so that she could no longer make out the
words. Kendrick couldn't marry Melissa. She wasn't at all
right for him. She would surely be whiny and critical like her
mother. Poor Kendrick would lose all his sense of adventure
in no time.

Without deliberation, Glorianna began to change her
clothes. As she struggled to fasten the buttons on her riding
habit, confusion reigned. She needed to be alone and focus
on this problem. Since she did her best thinking on long
horse rides, she would saddle up Nina. She brushed aside
Conlon's caution about riding alone. She wouldn't be gone
long. What could a short ride hurt?

❧

As evening drew on, Glorianna waited until the soldiers
turned the other way, then she slipped out of the camp, hoping to be hidden by the brush and growing dusk. Getting this
far without being seen hadn't been difficult. Most people
were indoors preparing for supper. The wind whipped across
the desert in a hot, dry wave.

Nina, normally a sweet-tempered mare, wasn't happy
about being out. She had not wanted to leave her sweet hay
and the comforts of her stall. She fought the bit, trying to
turn toward home each time Glorianna relaxed her grip on
the reins. If she hadn't been such an experienced horse-
woman, she knew they wouldn't have gotten this far. For
safety, she urged Nina to take the road to Yuma. Wider than
the trail to the river, this road would lessen her chances of
getting lost.

"Nina, I have to figure a way to get back east to Kendrick."

Nina's ears flickered and she snorted.

"Don't you start in on me, too. I'm telling you Kendrick is
wonderful. That's why all the girls like him, isn't it?"

Nina pranced on without comment.

Could she be wrong about him? Glorianna relaxed her grip on the reins as she pondered her decision to marry Kendrick. She'd wanted this for so long that she couldn't remember her original reason for deciding to marry him. He was handsome, but so were a lot of men, especially Conlon. She frowned. Where had that thought come from?

Could her father be right? Was Kendrick's penchant for changing jobs due to his shiftlessness? Would he care for a wife and family properly? Should she wait and see what happened or should she do her best to get back home?

The low rumble of thunder startled her. "How did it get so dark, Girl?" She patted the horse's neck. "We'd better get back. That storm looks like it means business."

Glorianna swung the mare around. She had no idea how long she'd been riding, but Camp MacDowell couldn't be too far.

A flash of lightning lit up the black sky. Rain-laden clouds lumbered closer. A crack of thunder shook the ground. Nina jumped, then spooked again as the wind peppered them with debris from the ground. Glorianna worked hard to hold the frightened mare steady. Her nervous prancing took them sideways down the road.

Glorianna squinted against the wind. Hidden in blackness, the road was difficult to see, much less follow, until an occasional flash of lightning illuminated the desert. She searched the countryside for shelter during those brief moments of light. The flat landscape held no hope of refuge. Gnarled mesquite trees and prickly cactus offered no protection from the intensity of the storm. Where had this storm come from so fast?

She longed to urge Nina into a canter, hoping there would be something up ahead, something to block out the wind and the inevitable rain. Nina spooked constantly, afraid of every lightning flash and boom of thunder. Glorianna knew she shouldn't have left the camp when she did. Most of all she regretted going alone.

Had she lost the road? There weren't any high spots near here so that she could get her bearings. What if she found no shelter? Would anyone find her in this desolate place? A growing fear threatened to overtake her.

Unbidden, Conlon's face came to mind. She smiled and relaxed slightly as she remembered the comforting feel of his arms around her. She knew the look in his brilliant blue eyes as he gazed at her. He loved her. She tried to push thoughts of him away, for she knew he wasn't God's plan for her, even if Conlon believed he was. But, Glorianna knew with certainty that if she got lost, Conlon would find her. No matter how bad the storm, no matter how far from the road she strayed, he would come for her.

The first of the rain spattered in huge drops against her cheeks. She hunched over the saddle, urging Nina to go faster. They must be getting close to the camp and to shelter. She wasn't prepared for the hard-hitting deluge that dropped from the sky. Lightning seared the clouds; thunder rocked the heavens, and a curtain of rain descended that cut everything else off.

Nina reared and jumped sideways, throwing Glorianna off balance. The rain-soaked desert floor, slippery as ice, gave way beneath the mare's hooves. Nina crashed to the ground. Glorianna flew from the saddle, her head connecting with a rock. Darkness enveloped her.

❧

"Lieutenant Sullivan!" Captain Wilton's roar as he slammed open the door to the officers' quarters made Conlon jump. He winced as the needle he held pierced his finger. He set down the shirt and button he'd been sewing and crossed the room.

"Yes, Sir." He snapped to attention.

Captain Wilton looked as if he had just realized how gruff he sounded. He sighed and ran his hand through his wind-rumpled hair. "I'm sorry, Sullivan. I didn't mean to sound like an angry bear." At Conlon's nod he continued, "Have you seen my daughter?"

Conlon frowned and shook his head. "I haven't seen her since this afternoon when I delivered a letter to her."

"Where was she then?"

"She had just helped Fayth carry home some purchases from the mercantile. She took the letter and went home. Why do you ask?"

An uncharacteristic look of fear clouded the captain's eyes. "She's disappeared. She isn't home or at the Holwells'."

"Did you ask Maria?"

"Yes, she hasn't seen her for a couple of hours. She had to go to the mercantile and when she returned, Glorianna was gone."

Conlon reached over to the peg by the door where his cap hung. "Let's go see what we can find out."

The wind blew against them and made walking a chore as they crossed the open area to the captain's house. In order to be heard, Conlon shouted at the captain. "Did you check with the other women?"

Captain Wilton nodded. "None of them have seen her this afternoon. The wind and blowing sand kept everyone indoors." He paused and waited until they stepped into the house to continue. "Glorianna knows what time you eat supper. I can't imagine where she is."

"Did you ask Fayth what she thought? She and your daughter have become good friends."

"She said Glorianna helped her some this morning. Fayth says she was fine then."

"What about the letter? Could there have been bad news from back east?"

Captain Wilton frowned. "I don't know. I haven't seen any letter."

Conlon couldn't stand around any longer. An uneasy feeling settled in the pit of his stomach. He had to do something to find Glorianna before it was too late. Too late? He frowned at the thought.

"Why don't you check her room, Sir? See if you can find

that letter. I'll talk to Maria again."

The clip of his boot heels echoed down the hall as the captain headed for his daughter's bedroom. Conlon crossed quietly to the kitchen, trying to ignore the growling of his stomach when the rich aromas of simmering vegetables hit.

"Maria?" The petite Mexican girl turned at his call. "We're trying to find Glorianna. Have you noticed anything that might help?"

Maria broke off a piece of dough and began shaping a small tortilla before she answered. "*Sí, Señor,*" she said, hesitantly. "I think something might help." She spoke rapidly in Spanish then stopped suddenly, looking embarrassed. "Sorry," she said. "Forget speaking English sometimes."

"That's okay." Conlon forced a smile, trying to put the nervous girl at ease. He wanted to pick her up and shake her. "Just tell me anything you can."

"Señorita's riding clothes gone, *Señor.*"

"Her clothes?" Conlon glanced around at the ironing board in the corner of the kitchen.

"I washed yesterday. Today I iron. Her riding clothes were here. Now they gone."

"Thank you, Maria." Conlon turned and headed out of the kitchen toward the bedroom. A sense of impending doom weighed heavily on him.

"Lieutenant, come here." Captain Wilton looked grim as he strode out of Glorianna's room, a piece of paper fluttering in his hand. "Apparently, Sullivan, my daughter did receive bad news. At least, it's bad to her."

"What is it, Sir?" Conlon reached impatiently for the letter, but the captain pulled it away.

"I can't let you read it, Sullivan. The letter is personal. Believe me, though, I know she's upset. The man she wanted to go back and marry is getting married to a girl Glorianna despises. There's no telling where she's gone."

Conlon raced across the parade ground to the stables, ignoring the grit of sand in his eyes. The sweet scent of rain hung heavy in the air. Foreboding built inside him like the massive clouds overhead.

Nina's stall was empty. Conlon stared for a moment as reality sank in. Glorianna had gone riding. She would be caught in this storm.

"What did you find, Sullivan?" Captain Wilton strode toward him down the center aisle of the stables.

"Her horse is gone, Sir." Conlon hated the look of fear in the captain's eyes. He knew his thoughts were on the storm and his daughter braving the elements. "I'll go after her, Captain. I'll bring her back."

Captain Wilton placed his hand on Conlon's shoulder. His voice sounded husky against the rising howl of the wind. "Find her for me, Sullivan. She's all I have. She doesn't understand these desert storms."

ঽ৯

Conlon had barely enough time to decipher which road Glorianna had taken before the rain swept out of the skies. Champ pranced momentarily, then calmed down and slogged ahead through the wind, rain, and slippery desert.

She's on the road to Yuma, he thought. *Does she think she can return home and win her boyfriend back? God, I don't understand this. Please, keep her safe. Help me to find her.*

Lightning struck a nearby mesquite tree. The resulting thunderclap vibrated the air around them. Champ reared, startled by the brilliant flash and loud noise. Conlon brought him down easily then leaned to run his hand down the horse's wet neck. He did his best to soothe the trembling beast.

Hours seemed to pass before the rain eased up to a slow, steady shower, yet Conlon knew it hadn't been that long. He strained to see through the moonless night. Champ lifted his head and nickered softly. Conlon leaned forward trying to see. He wished for one more flash of lightning to illuminate the night.

A movement ahead caught his attention. Out of the darkness, Nina's soft whinny reached them. By the next flash, they saw her. She stood, her reins held fast among some rocks, her left front hoof lifted off the ground. Conlon swung down from Champ and approached the mare, dread making him shake.

"Easy, girl." He ran his hands over the drenched horse. The mud caked on her knees told of her fall. Her foreleg was tender, but he couldn't feel any sign of lasting damage. He couldn't feel any sticky blood on the saddle, as he ran his hands across it.

"Where's Glorianna, girl?"

Conlon stepped around the horse. His eyes strained against the inky blackness. *Please, God, help me find her,* he begged again. As if in answer to his prayer, lightning flashed, and the image of her crumpled body was forever burned into his memory.

eight

Dear God, no. Conlon wanted to call out. His throat constricted in fear, and he only mouthed the words that his mind screamed. In two long strides he reached her side. He knelt by her rain-drenched form.

"Glorianna," his voice cracked. She didn't move. The rain and the fall had loosened her long braid. He swept the sodden curls back from her face. Her pale skin shone in the blackness. She didn't move, didn't appear to breathe.

Oh, God, please, let her be all right. Don't let her die like this. A slight movement caught his eye. He reached down and slipped his fingers around her slender, cold hand. Ever so slowly, her fingers tightened around his. Tears trickled down his cheeks, lost amidst the raindrops. Conlon's head bent forward. *Thank You, Lord. Thank You.*

Conlon hurried back to Champ and retrieved the extra rain slicker and blanket he had thought to bring with him. Placing the blanket over Glorianna's still form, he put the slicker over that. He hoped she would be able to warm up a little. Her fingers and cheeks were like ice. He wondered if it was due to her being soaked and the drop in temperature, or from her injuries.

Gently, he checked for broken bones, trying to determine how badly she had been hurt in the fall. As he ran his hand over her head, he felt the lump and the rock she rested against. Now he knew why she lay so still.

She groaned. He leaned closer to her. "Glorianna? Can you hear me?"

Her eyelids fluttered. Her forehead puckered and her eyelids twitched again. They quivered once more, then opened slightly.

"Don't try to talk, Sweetheart. I'm going to take you back to the camp. I'll do my best not to hurt you."

She tried to nod. Her face paled even more at the effort. Then, her eyes drifted shut again. Conlon wanted to lift her into his arms and comfort her. He wanted to take away her pain and make her well, but it wasn't in his power. Instead, he went to bring the horses closer. He tied Nina's reins to Champ's saddle, then returned to Glorianna.

Cradling her head in his arms, Conlon rewrapped the blanket and slicker around her. She weighed almost nothing. He pulled her close. The faint scent of roses wafted around him. He pressed his cheek to hers, willing her to be okay, to be strong for the ride back to camp. The storm had eased. Moonlight pierced through the clouds and chased away the inky darkness.

Champ seemed to understand the need to walk. Nina hobbled beside them. Glorianna rested against Conlon's chest. Her breathing was even and a faint flush tinted her cheeks. He prayed it wasn't the start of a fever, but her true color coming back.

Swaying in the saddle with the rhythm of Champ's walk, Conlon gazed down at Glorianna. Her long, dark eyelashes rested on creamy white cheeks. Her petite nose turned up slightly. Rosebud lips curled in a secret smile, making him long to brush them with his own.

He had to do something to distract his thoughts, so he began to talk, even though he knew she couldn't hear him. "Glorianna," he whispered. "You are well named. You are a glory to look at." He paused, smiled, then continued. "In fact, I believe from now on I'll call you Glory. Every time I do, you will remind me of the glory of God and how He made you for me. I know you don't believe me about that, but it's true." Conlon reached up and brushed a lock of hair from her face. "For years, I've prayed for you. I asked God to give me a wife like my mother." He laughed softly. "I didn't know you would be as feisty."

He smiled. "You see, my mother is tiny, just like you. She has the same red hair and fiery temper. I learned at a young age not to cross her." He paused a moment, swallowing a lump in his throat. "But the thing I loved most about my mother was her love for my dad. She loved him with everything in her. And she loved God the same way."

He leaned forward and pressed his lips lightly on Glorianna's temple. "I want you to love me like that, Glory. I think you already do, you just haven't realized it yet. Most of all, I want you to follow God's will."

"As for the man back east you think you want," Conlon clenched his teeth, trying to keep the anger from his voice, "Remember this, Glory, if he passed you by for that other girl, then he isn't worth the bother. You deserve better."

With a sigh, he pulled her even closer, trying to keep her warm. The wind had died down and the rain had slowed, but she was wet clear through. Champ's pricked ears told him they were nearing Camp MacDowell.

He gazed down at her, his fingers trailing down her cheek. He leaned forward slightly, giving in to temptation and followed the path of his fingers with one of light kisses. He sighed. "I love you so much, Sweetheart. Please don't make me wait forever, although I will, if need be."

Arriving at Camp MacDowell, Conlon roused the guard with a shout. A cavalryman ran to take Nina's reins from him. "Rub her down and tend to her leg," Conlon said. "Send someone for the doctor. I'll take Miss Wilton to her house."

At the sound of hoofbeats, the door to Glorianna's house flung open. Her father, Fayth, and Timothy stood framed in the light. "I have her, Sir."

"Thank God." Captain Wilton rushed from the house. "Is she okay?"

Leaning forward to hand Glorianna to her father, Conlon found himself reluctant to let her go. "Be careful. Her horse fell with her. She hit her head on a rock and hasn't regained consciousness, except for a moment."

Fayth let out a cry, her hand quickly covering her mouth as she looked at Glorianna's still form. "Bring her in. Hurry. We need to get these wet things off her. I'll get Maria to help me. Conlon, did you get the doctor?"

Without waiting for his answer, she rushed into the house ahead of the captain.

ða

Light pierced her eyes, like a dagger stabbing through to the back of her head. She snapped them shut and held them there tightly. Maybe if she refused to let her eyelids open, this blinding pain would go away. Glorianna tried to breathe in shallow breaths, hoping to settle the churning in her stomach. Her efforts didn't work.

She inched her eyelids apart. The light didn't hurt quite as much, but the ache was still too much to bear. She closed them and relaxed slightly. She now knew she was in her bedroom, lying in bed. How had she gotten here? The last thing she remembered was the lightning and thunder and Nina's rearing in terror.

Booted feet clunked across the floor. Why were they stomping so hard? Couldn't whoever it was walk a little more softly? She would tell them.

"Are you awake?" The note of concern in Conlon's voice almost made her smile. Then, she remembered she needed to tell him to walk quietly before he stomped holes in the floor.

Glorianna opened her eyes and attempted to sit. Conlon knelt by her bed and reached for her hand. Too late she knew she had made a mistake. Before she could turn away, her stomach emptied itself all over her, the bed, and the man who claimed to love her. Horrified, Glorianna dropped back on the bed. As everything faded into darkness once more, she knew she would never be able to face him again.

The next time Glorianna awoke, pale moonlight illuminated the room. She eased her eyes open, hoping her memory of throwing up on Conlon had only been a dream. *A nightmare, actually,* she thought. The pounding in her head had eased and her stomach felt more settled than it had earlier.

"Kitten?"

She turned her head toward her father. She wondered if the smile she forced looked more like a grimace than a smile. "Hi," she rasped, her voice not cooperating with her. "How long have I been asleep?"

Her father leaned close. "You've slept for two days now. We were pretty worried. The doctor said there was nothing to do but wait."

She tried to nod. A cool night breeze brought the scent of rain to her. "Did it rain again?"

"We got a little monsoon tonight. Not like the other one, though."

She closed her eyes to shut out the pain written in her father's gaze. "I'm sorry. I wanted time to think. I didn't know the storm would come so fast."

"It's okay, Kitten. The weather here takes some getting used to."

She tried to nod and tell him she might have been wrong, but her head began pounding again. She closed her eyes and barely heard the scrape of the chair accompanied by her father's whispered, "Good night," before drifting back to sleep.

"Good morning, sleepyhead." Fayth's cheerful voice and the tread of her steps in the bedroom made Glorianna wince.

"Good morning." The words rasped in her ears.

"Maria tells me you haven't eaten much of anything." Fayth settled into the chair next to the bed. "I have her fixing some broth. I want you to try your best to eat." She grinned. "I hope to keep you from throwing up on me like you did on Conlon. I don't think he's recovered yet."

"Every time I try to eat, I get sick to my stomach. I don't have any appetite yet."

"It's been four days since Conlon brought you in looking like a drowned rat. We need to get you well." Fayth leaned forward and brushed the hair away from Glorianna's forehead.

"Today, we'll try a little harder." She smiled to soften her words. "I think we need to start with some serious prayer about your health and about that gentleman that made you ride off alone."

"Why should we pray about Kendrick?"

Fayth sighed. "I don't know why you're so determined to marry him. Can you tell me?"

"Because it's what God wants."

"How do you know?"

Glorianna stirred restlessly in the bed. For some reason Fayth's question made her uneasy. "I guess, I just feel it. He's so handsome and fun loving. I'm sure he's perfect for me."

"You know, it isn't wise to trust our feelings unless we can back it up with God's Word."

"What do you mean by that?" Glorianna stared at the ceiling, trying to avoid Fayth's knowing gaze.

"Have you checked to see what God thinks about Kendrick's attributes?"

"God loves everyone. I'm sure He loves Kendrick, too."

Fayth frowned. "Of course, God loves us all," Fayth agreed. "However, God hates sin, and He doesn't want us to be unequally yoked with someone who doesn't know Him in the same way we do."

"Kendrick goes to church sometimes." The defense sounded lame.

"But does he put God first in his life? Will he put God first in your marriage?" Fayth lifted Glorianna's hand from the covers and squeezed it lightly. "These are questions you need to pray about. Only you can find the answers."

Glorianna listened in silence as Fayth prayed for God to give her wisdom in the decision she needed to make. A lump settled in her throat and she realized that maybe, just maybe, she wanted to marry Kendrick so desperately that she assumed God wanted it, too. How did Fayth know what God wanted if she didn't go by feelings?

Maria entered the room quietly, carrying a tray. The smell

of broth drifted across the room. For the first time, Glorianna felt a faint stirring of hunger. Perhaps good health wasn't so far away after all.

After eating as much as she could hold, Glorianna listened to Fayth talk about Alyce and her latest antics. When she couldn't hold her eyes open any longer, she heard Fayth whisper that she would be back later.

≥⋅

The early morning chill felt refreshing after the scorching desert days. The sky softened slowly from dark gray to deep blue. Conlon breathed in the fresh, crisp air, looking forward to the special time he shared every day with God. Arizona sunrises were God's handiwork at its best.

A family of jackrabbits browsed through the brush looking for the most succulent plants to nibble. Their long ears waved in the breeze. Extra large hind legs made them look as if they were ready to topple over on their noses. Conlon grinned at the thought. He wasn't sure how a coyote ever caught one of the fleet-footed rabbits.

He turned his face to the sky and noted the clouds building already. It would probably rain again today. He frowned. There were rumors of Apache uprisings. The captain might send a troop to scout around the Superstition Mountains. He hoped he didn't have to go with them, but he felt certain he would.

"God," he whispered, "the truth is I don't want to be away from Glorianna. I don't want to shirk my duty, either, but I feel so protective of her."

Seven days had passed since he brought her home that stormy night. The feeling of holding her in his arms had haunted him ever since. "I love her so much, Lord. What am I supposed to do?"

The sky lightened and the first faint traces of color began to form among the clouds. "God, I know Josiah says I should be patient. He keeps quoting from Psalm 37, *Rest in the Lord, and wait patiently for Him.*" He sighed, a sound wrenched from deep in his soul. "I don't know how long I can rest, Lord. Help me to be patient with her today. Maybe if I take it one day at a time it will be easier."

He picked up a rock and flung it in the direction of the grazing rabbits. They bounded away across the desert faster than one might imagine possible.

"I haven't even seen her since the day after I brought her home. She won't allow me in or talk to me at all." He kicked at a rock, sending it skittering away. "I don't know if she's embarrassed or if she won't ever want to see me again. She can't hide forever.

"Should I forget her, Lord? Please don't say I should. I know I couldn't on my own. But if Your will is that I not marry her, then give me the strength to accept it." Conlon hung his head. A feeling of despair threatened to destroy his early morning ritual.

As if God were ready to talk, a brilliant display of colors washed across the eastern sky. Pinks, purples, and gold blended with the blue, painting a dazzling picture. He looked up and smiled through the glittering tears in his eyes. Only God could do this kind of artwork.

"Oh!" The gasp from behind him startled Conlon. Had someone been listening to his private conversation with God? He whirled around, then stared in astonishment.

nine

"Glorianna!"

As Conlon closed the gap between them in two quick strides, she tore her gaze from the colors rippling across the sky to focus on him. He swept her into his arms, crushing her in a fierce hug. "I'm so glad to see you up and around, Sweetheart."

His blue eyes, darker in the morning light, held her fast. His earthy scent washed over her, and her heart began to pound. He lowered his head, his lips coming closer to hers. For a fleeting breath of time, Glorianna wanted to feel his lips on hers, to be swept away by his kiss. Instead, she turned her head and his lips brushed her cheek. She struggled against him, but he seemed oblivious. "Lieutenant." She pushed him. "Lieutenant, let me go!"

Glorianna freed one hand. Swinging as hard as she could in such close confines, she slapped his cheek. He stepped back from the embrace, a look of surprise and confusion clouding his eyes.

She stepped back to put some distance between them. Her body, taut with emotion, felt like a leaf in the wind. "Lieutenant, I am not your sweetheart. Neither did I come out here for your pleasure. In fact, I heard you mumbling to yourself and was leaving."

"I was praying."

"I couldn't make out the words. I didn't mean to intrude."

He studied her for a moment. His features relaxed slightly as if he was relieved about something, but she didn't know what. She tried to calm her breathing, hoping her cheeks weren't as red as they felt. "Why did you come out here?"

Her face burned at the thought of his thinking she came

looking for him. "I couldn't sleep. I wanted to get some air and think. Now, if you'll excuse me, I'll get back."

She turned before he could say more and walked back toward the camp, forcing herself not to run. Tears crowded together in her eyes and threatened to overflow. Dashing at them angrily with the back of her hand, she headed for the stables. Maybe a talk with Nina would help sort out her confused feelings about Conlon.

The stables were quiet. Most of the horses were resting. Nina's soft nicker comforted her when she leaned over the stall. The mare limped as she moved to the door. Dirty smudges covered the wrap on her leg. Glorianna made a mental note to put on a fresh bandage today.

"Good morning, girl," she whispered as she stroked the soft, questing nose. "I didn't bring you a treat, but I'll see that you get one later today. How's your leg?"

"I believe that leg is gonna be fine, Miss Wilton." Josiah Washington's booming voice echoed through the stables, eliciting a startled cry from Glorianna.

"Mr. Washington," she gasped. "I didn't know you were here."

"I like to get an early start on the day." The blacksmith grinned at her. "I came to check out some of the horses, like that pretty little mare of yours. Her leg is mending right nice."

Glorianna relaxed. Nina nudged her, demanding more attention. She wanted to bury her face in the mare's neck and cry. What did the Lord want from her? Why couldn't she have the peace Fayth spoke of having? Inner turmoil had her stomach in knots. She turned her head away and hoped Josiah hadn't seen the tear that trickled down her cheek.

"Are you all right?" Josiah's soft voice reflected his concern.

"I'm fine." She nearly choked on the lie. "I guess I'm just glad Nina wasn't hurt too bad when she fell."

Josiah chuckled, a deep rumbling sound like distant thunder. "I think you should be glad Lieutenant Sullivan found you."

Swiping away the tear, Glorianna looked up at the huge blacksmith. "What do you mean?"

"I mean, it was crazy to be out in that storm. You were off the road in the desert. I believe only a miracle from God made him notice you."

"But, I was careful to stay on the road."

"Maybe you were careful, but it was dark and stormy. I'll bet Nina wasn't calm and sweet like usual, was she?"

"She was a little edgy," Glorianna admitted. "But, then, I'm an experienced rider."

Josiah's grin lit up the stables. "Conlon told me you're a good rider, Ma'am, but, I'll tell you something. There isn't another man in this company who would have risked his life riding after you in that storm."

Glorianna wanted to run from the truth he forced her to see. She had put another person's life in danger.

"Conlon loves you, Miss Wilton." Josiah studied her, speaking softly. "I hope you at least thanked him for saving your life. Good day."

Glorianna watched him leave as she reflected on the elements of nature gone crazy during that horrendous storm. Why would anyone want to be out in that unless he had a mission for the person he loved or thought he loved? She had done some deep soul-searching in the past few days and knew she had been wrong about Kendrick. Now she must wait for God to show her His will for her life. Was Conlon the answer?

Lost in thought, she nervously clasped and unclasped her hands as she made her way back outside the camp. Would he still be there? Would he even want to see her? What would she say to him?

She quietly wove through the prickly desert plants. The brilliant colors had faded from the sky, leaving it a pale, washed-out blue. Conlon sat on the rock, his back toward her. His head rested in his hands; a look of utter dejection and defeat surrounded him. Glorianna stopped, overwhelmed by the need to run to him and feel his embrace.

&

Conlon heard footsteps behind him. *Oh, God, make them go away. I can't face anyone right now. Why did I do that? Why couldn't I see that she doesn't love me? She has no idea how she haunts my every thought. I can't sleep if I don't see her each night. Every day I look forward to being around her. This last week has been awful without her. When I saw her standing there, I couldn't help myself. I just had to hold her. Now she'll hate me. Lord, help me to trust You. Show me what to do.*

"Conlon?"

He froze. Had he heard Glorianna call his name or was he imagining things? She never called him Conlon. Hesitantly, almost afraid of what he would find, Conlon stood up and swung around.

It was Glorianna. She looked like an angel. The pale yellow dress danced lightly in the breeze. Her red hair shone with the sun's highlights. Her pale cheeks accented the brightness of her green eyes and ruby lips.

He tried to speak. His mouth opened, but nothing came out. Why had she come back?

Glorianna licked her lips. Her hands were clasped in front of her. "I want to thank you."

Thank him? She wanted to thank him? He never expected her to say something like that. Why was she thanking him? For mauling her? Because he was such a stupid oaf? He couldn't seem to find his tongue to ask.

She took a step toward him. "I want to thank you for saving my life. I didn't mean to put you in danger when I went riding last week. I didn't know the storm would come so fast." She rambled on as if unable to stem the flow of words now that they were started.

When she paused to catch her breath, he gestured toward the rock. "Would you like to join me? The sunrise colors are gone, but maybe we could just talk until time for breakfast."

She nodded, then went over and eased herself onto the rock.

He sat beside her, careful not to come too close, although he longed to wrap his arm around her. Her rose scent beckoned him, but he fought the temptation.

The moments stretched on in silence. There were a hundred things he wanted to ask her, but all of them were wrong. Would she ever be able to love him? Did she still love Kendrick? Could she be happy married to a cavalryman? He couldn't ask any of them. So he kept his peace.

"I hear you love horses." She broke the silence.

He looked at her, nearly losing himself in her liquid green eyes. "Some day I'd like to raise horses." He smiled, as the dream took shape once again in his mind. "Not just any breed, either. They have to be the best."

"And where do you intend to raise these horses of yours?"

"I've been up north in Arizona. There's some of the best pastureland I've ever seen in those mountains. I could raise some fine horses there." The picture of mountain pastures and towering pines was so real he could almost feel the cool air and see the horses grazing in grass up to their knees.

A light touch on his arm brought him out of his reverie. Glorianna quickly withdrew her hand as he smiled down at her. "It sounds like a beautiful dream." She returned his smile, causing his heart to pound. "I can almost see it from your description."

The clear notes of a bugle brought him back to the present. "I have to get back to camp and so do you. Your father will worry if he can't find you." He stood and offered his hand to help her up. She hesitated then placed her small fingers into his hand. Once again, he fought a battle to keep from pulling her into his arms.

"I come here every morning. If you find you can't sleep, you're welcome to join me."

"I just might do that." She smiled once again, her countenance rivaling the beauty of the sunrise.

❧

At the Verde River, Glorianna laughed at Alyce as the little girl put her face in the water, then came up chortling while it dripped off her nose and chin. She had never seen a young child enjoy the water as much as Alyce did. They had to guard her constantly because she showed no fear of the river.

Laughing, she reached out to hug Alyce. Fayth hadn't been feeling well. She stayed home, and Glorianna promised to watch Alyce. She really wanted to give Fayth some time to rest without the active toddler to oversee. Alyce made the whole bathing trip more fun, anyway.

Settling the laughing girl in her lap, Glorianna's thoughts drifted as Alyce played. Conlon and the other men were downriver, washing and cooling off. She sighed, thinking of the morning talks she and Conlon had shared in the past few weeks. They had come to enjoy their quiet time watching the sun change the sky from dark to brilliant color.

She remembered what Fayth said about checking for the qualities God would want her to look for in a man. Conlon had those qualities. Every morning he shared something new and exciting he had learned about God. He loved to read the Bible, and his greatest regret came from there being no formal gathering of Christians in the area. He missed his church.

They had begun to share their hopes and dreams with one another. At first, Glorianna was hesitant, thinking Conlon would become impatient and forward. She had been wrong. He modeled gentility. Sometimes she could see the desire to touch her in his eyes, but he always refrained as if waiting for her to signal her readiness.

Every day she liked him more. Liked him? She wasn't sure if that was the right term anymore. Did she love him? She loved his devotion to the Lord. She loved the way his eyes sparkled with humor. She loved his joking. She loved to look at his handsome face when she thought he wouldn't notice. Come to think of it, there was quite a lot she loved about Conlon.

"Go'wy." Alyce tugged on Glorianna's clothes. "Out. Play there." She pointed at the shore.

Glorianna smiled. Alyce had trouble saying her name, but

it was so cute. Conlon sometimes mimicked the girl, but most of the time he called her "Glory." Kathleen was the only other one who had ever called her by that nickname.

"Okay, Sweetie, let's go." Glorianna picked Alyce up and headed for the path up to the wagons. They would dry off, then play peekaboo in the brush, Alyce's second favorite thing to do.

"Where are you?" Glorianna called after they had dried off. Alyce giggled loudly and Glorianna could barely keep from laughing. She could see the girl standing with her face toward a tree. Her hands covered her eyes, and she thought she was invisible. "Where are you?" Glorianna called again, biting her lip to stop the laughter.

"Peekboo." Alyce's deep chuckles were infectious. Glorianna couldn't believe how much the girl had changed in the last few months. Her second birthday was only two months away, and every day she acted more like a little girl than a baby.

Alyce churned her chubby little legs into action as she headed into the brush to hide once more. "Wait, Alyce, don't go far."

Glorianna hurried after her, ducking around a gnarled mesquite tree. Alyce stood with her hands covering her face, waiting for Glorianna to look for her. A low buzzing noise filled the air. A remembered fear stopped Glorianna.

Frozen in place, she looked for the source of the noise. Under the bush beside Alyce, a rattlesnake lay coiled, his spade-shaped head poised to strike. Glorianna didn't know what to do. If she screamed for help, Alyce might get scared and move.

She had no gun to shoot with, but looking at the ground, she noticed a small rock beside her foot. Ever so slowly, she stretched down for the stone. With its weight in her hand she straightened, trying to pray, remembering that David defeated a giant with one stone and the Lord. *Please, God, help me,* she prayed, hoping He could direct her aim.

As soon as the rock left her hand, Glorianna leapt forward to snatch Alyce away before the snake could strike. Her aim wasn't quite true. The rock missed the snake's head, thudding into its coiled body. The rattler's head darted at Alyce's leg. Glorianna jerked her up and jumped back. The girl's scream told her she hadn't been fast enough.

A gunshot echoed along the riverbank. The snake exploded and Glorianna whirled away in revulsion. Conlon grabbed her and pulled her out of the brush.

"Did she get bit?" he asked, roughly.

Glorianna didn't have to look to know something was wrong. Alyce screamed and twisted in her arms.

"Hold her still while I check her," Conlon ordered.

Trembling, Glorianna tried to obey. Alyce threw herself from side to side, resisting their efforts to help her. Glorianna knew she needed to be calm in order to keep the girl quiet.

"It's okay, Sweetie," she crooned. "It's okay." She smoothed the hair back from Alyce's forehead, praying for the girl.

From the corner of her eye she watched as Conlon removed Alyce's shoe. Briefly, he worked on the leg, then went to a nearby mud hole. He brought back a handful of mud and slathered it over Alyce's lower leg.

Conlon looked up at her, his face grim. "We have to get her back to camp. I've done what I can, but she'll need to see the doctor."

Glorianna's mouth felt like cotton. She tried to speak, but nothing came out. Tears burned in her eyes. How had this happened? Fayth had trusted her to watch over Alyce and now she might die. Fayth would never forgive her for this.

ten

Numbness settled over Glorianna as Conlon lifted Alyce from her arms. As though enveloped in a dense fog, she heard the shouts and cries of the men and women who raced up from the river to see what happened. She still knelt on the ground as confusion reigned.

She tried to listen to Conlon as he spoke with Timothy about his daughter. His deep voice soothed her, but she could only pick up a word here and there. Conversation about the snake, Alyce's shoe, and the doctor drifted past. Some of the women tried to talk to her, but Glorianna couldn't answer. Grief and guilt consumed her.

Loud creaking grated on her nerves. The mules strained to pull the ambulance back to the camp. The thunder of hooves told her someone was hurrying to the camp to alert the doctor and Fayth. Soon it would start. Fayth would hear the news, and they would no longer be friends. Tears began to slide down her cheeks, splatting unheeded on her folded hands.

"Glory?" Conlon squatted on the ground in front of her. "Sweetheart, she's going to be okay."

He reached out and lifted her hands in his, wiping the tears from them. Holding her hands fast in one hand, he touched her wet cheek with the other. His fingers traced the path of her tears. Glorianna closed her eyes and welcomed his soothing touch.

Taking her chin in his hand, Conlon lifted until her eyes met his. His blue eyes were filled with compassion. She wanted so much for him to hold her, but she knew what she had done made her unworthy. She closed her eyes again to shut out the pain.

"Glory, look at me."

She couldn't.

"She's going to be okay, you know."

Glorianna's eyes flew open. "Alyce?" she whispered, as if hearing him for the first time. "How do you know?"

Seated on the ground, Conlon pulled her close, letting her lean on him. "When you hit the snake with the rock, its aim changed. Then you grabbed Alyce. When the snake struck, it hit her shoe."

"Then she didn't really get bit?" Glorianna swung around to face Conlon. She held her breath, hoping it was true.

"Oh, she got bit all right."

Her hopes sank as quickly as they had risen.

"But, it was a grazing bite."

She searched his eyes for a reason to hope. "Will she. . . does that mean. . .?"

"I'm sure she'll be just fine." Conlon's smile felt like a balm to her wounded soul. "She'll be a little sick and her leg will hurt, but that should be all. Fayth will need your help."

Glorianna stood and turned away, crossing her arms over her stomach. "Fayth won't want to see me ever again."

Conlon stood, put his arms around her, and pulled her against him again. "Now why would you say that? Fayth thinks you're wonderful."

"Don't you see?" She whirled around, anger making her words loud. "She trusted me with her child and I betrayed that trust." Tears of self-directed anger and shame washed down her cheeks.

Conlon grabbed her. His eyes darkened. "Don't you realize you saved her life? If you hadn't thought and acted so quickly Alyce would be dead. This wasn't your fault."

"Yes, it was." She tried to back away from him. He pulled her against his chest, embracing her. She gripped his shirt in her hands and sobbed. "Every time I'm supposed to take care of someone, she dies. Alyce will die just like my mother did."

"Oh, Sweetheart." Conlon tenderly tightened his hold, his cheek pressed against her head, one hand softly rubbing her back. When her sobs quieted, he spoke. "Your father told me about your mother. It wasn't your fault she died. There was nothing you could have done to prevent it. Your father doesn't blame you. If anything, he's struggled with his own guilt for having left you in charge when he knew she was dying."

He lifted her chin, placing a tender kiss on her forehead. "Come with me now and talk to Fayth. She will understand."

Glorianna nodded, wondering why this man had the ability to comfort her like no other person could. She thought she would be happy to stay forever in his embrace.

❧

Glorianna smoothed her dress with shaky fingers as she approached the Holwell house with Conlon. Conlon had sent one of the men with the ambulance, keeping his horse for her to ride. During the ride back from the river, she hoped fervently Alyce would be okay and that Fayth would find it in her heart to forgive. *Oh, please help her forgive me. I don't think I can bear to lose her as a friend.*

Timothy swung the door open, grinned, and beckoned them in. "Fayth," he called. "They're here."

Before Glorianna had time to be afraid, Timothy engulfed her in a hug. Then Fayth was there, crying, thanking her, and holding her as if she would never let go.

"I don't know how I can thank you enough." Fayth stepped back, her hands still holding Glorianna's. "You saved my little girl, and all I can do is say thank you."

She turned to Conlon and hugged him. "Thank you, too. The doctor said that you helped by having the foresight to put fresh mud on the bite."

Glorianna barely knew when Conlon wrapped his arm around her. Exhaustion made her want to lie down and sleep right then. Elation made her want to sing and dance. She'd been forgiven. She didn't understand why, but she knew Fayth still wanted her as a friend.

"I have to get back to Alyce." Fayth turned back to Glorianna and hugged her again. "You look worn out. Why don't you get some sleep and come by tomorrow. Alyce will want see you, I'm sure."

Numbly, Glorianna nodded and allowed Conlon to lead her home. Twilight settled over the desert. Crickets sang and, in the distance, coyotes raised their voices in a motley chorus. Peace wrapped around her like a soft blanket as Conlon pulled her once more into his embrace.

"Get some sleep, Glory." His husky whisper sent a tingle through her. "I can't wait to see you in the morning." He kissed her forehead and disappeared in the dusky evening.

❧

The next morning, Glorianna stuck her head through the Holwells' door. "Fayth?" She didn't want to call loudly and risk waking Fayth or Alyce if they were sleeping. She waited a moment, listening. A faint sound of singing drifted through the house. She smiled. Fayth loved to sing to Alyce. She said it helped her sleep.

Glorianna tiptoed across to Alyce's room and peeked through the door. Alyce's eyes were closed, her eyelashes dark against her pale cheeks. Fayth stroked her daughter's head and crooned a song about Jesus being her friend.

Fayth looked up and smiled at Glorianna, beckoning her to enter the room.

"Sit down." Fayth patted the chair beside her. "She's finally asleep. It's been a rough night for her."

Alyce looked frail and vulnerable in the morning light. Fayth, too, seemed drawn and tired.

"Did you get any sleep last night?"

Fayth smiled. "Timothy watched her for awhile so I could rest. You'll find out when you're a mother, though, that it's impossible to sleep when your child is sick or in pain."

Glorianna bit her lip, trying to swallow the lump closing her throat. She didn't want to cry again. "I'm so sorry this happened. I don't know how you could forgive me."

"What?" Fayth's eyes widened. "Why would there be anything to forgive? You saved Alyce's life when you grabbed her away like that."

"But, I'm responsible for her being bit in the first place." Glorianna wiped angrily at her eyes. "I should have been more careful."

"Glorianna, listen to me." Fayth's smile faded. "You have treated my daughter like she was your own. You did not intend for that snake to bite her. It was an accident. How could you help that?"

"I don't know. I just feel like this is my fault. I was so scared I would lose you as a friend."

Fayth hugged her. "I can't begin to think of not having you for a friend. And I know Alyce would be lost without you to play with her. Besides," she smiled, "you have to help with the baby."

"What baby?" Glorianna frowned.

"Why, the baby I'm expecting." Fayth laughed. "That's why I've been so tired and sick lately."

Glorianna gasped. "A baby! Oh, that's so wonderful. I can't wait." She hugged Fayth with enthusiasm, then pulled back. "Now, I insist you let me sit with Alyce while you get some sleep. Just tell me what to do and I'll be fine."

Fayth nodded and gestured to a bottle and packet on the table. "We've made a poultice of vinegar and gun powder. If she wakes you can bathe her leg and put more of that on. It helps to draw out the poison."

"Fayth?"

"Yes?" Fayth turned back to look at Glorianna.

"I don't understand how you can still trust God so much in spite of all this."

"Because I know He has a plan for my life, for Timothy's, and even for Alyce's."

"But how do you know His plan is right?"

Fayth smiled and took Glorianna's hand in hers. "I know there have been times when I doubted God and His direction. But, I've learned that I can't depend on what I feel. I have to trust what God tells me in the Bible."

"And what does He tell you?" Glorianna whispered.

Tipping her head to one side, Fayth looked at Glorianna a moment. "One of my favorite bits of wisdom from the Bible is Proverbs 3:5 and 6. It says, *Trust in the Lord with all thine heart; and lean not unto thine own understanding. In all thy ways acknowledge him, and he shall direct thy paths.* You see, all I have to do is trust Him and God will take care of the rest."

Fayth squeezed her hand. "Does this questioning have to do with a certain handsome cavalry officer?"

Glorianna felt the heat of a blush in her cheeks. "I suppose so. But don't you say anything. Promise?"

At Fayth's nod, she continued. "When I'm with Conlon it feels so perfect. But, sometimes I'm confused about what's right. I can't really explain what I mean."

Fayth stood up, leaned over, and hugged her. "Keep asking God to lead you and He will. You'll know the right way when you have God's peace."

♦

Conlon held Champ's foot aloft as Josiah measured to see if the last shoe fit properly. "Not quite," Josiah announced, heading back to the forge. "I'll just need to bend this side in a little more."

Josiah thrust the horseshoe back into the red embers. Yellow flames licked eagerly at the metal, then died down. "I hear you had some excitement at the river yesterday."

Conlon shook his head. "I'm beginning to think there's something about Glorianna that attracts snakes. There was the one under her cot, the one at the river, and the worst snake of all, Dirk."

Josiah laughed. "At least that's one snake who won't be bothering her again. He's long gone."

"Well, the other two are even farther from reach. They're dead. Sometimes I agree with those who say the only good snake is a dead snake."

Josiah pulled the reddened horseshoe from the coals.

Placing it on the anvil, he studied the glowing metal, then began to pound. He plunged the shoe into water before walking back out to Champ with Conlon.

"I agree. I don't know why God allows some snakes to live." Josiah lifted Champ's foot and aligned the shoe. "But, we have to remember that God knows more than we'll ever know. You can trust Him with her. No matter how many critters are out there."

"You're right." Conlon grinned. "Here I am wanting to take over for God again."

Josiah laughed. "We all want to do that on occasion." He pounded the last of the nails into the horseshoe and dropped Champ's foot. "By the way, how's the problem with the future wife? Has she picked out her wedding dress yet?"

"You're asking for trouble." Conlon smiled. "It so happens that she's getting very fond of me. In fact, I think in no time at all I'll be able to ask her to marry me, and she'll jump at the chance."

Putting his tools away, Josiah smirked at Conlon. "You just may be in for a surprise. God has a way of taking us down a notch sometimes. I have a feeling you may be in for a rough time before your little filly agrees to a wedding."

"Exactly what have you heard?"

"Me? I haven't heard a thing. I just know God has a sense of humor. I'll be eagerly waiting to hear you say those vows. But I also know nothing has gone smoothly so far for the two of you."

Conlon started to lead Champ back to the stables. "Everything has changed, Josiah. You'll see," he called back.

❧

That evening, Timothy answered Conlon's knock and pulled him into the house. "Come in. I'm glad you could join us on such short notice."

Conlon smiled at Glorianna, seated across the room beside her father. "What's the occasion?" Conlon asked.

"Oh, good, you're all here." Fayth clapped her hands

together and peeked into Alyce's bedroom. "Alyce will be awake soon. Timothy, you tell them why we invited them."

"We thought we would celebrate Alyce's recovery." Timothy crossed the room and put his arm around Fayth. "We're so glad to have friends like you, and this is our way of saying thanks."

"I think Emily has the meal almost ready," Fayth said. "I'll check and be right back."

Conlon pulled a chair alongside Glorianna's and sat down. He wanted to take her hand in his, but refrained. The green dress she wore brought out the green in her eyes and accented the burnished copper of her hair. He longed to touch her again.

"Lieutenant Sullivan?" Captain Wilton pulled his attention from Glorianna. "Do you remember the Dentons?"

Conlon frowned at Timothy, whose face split in a huge grin. "I remember them," he admitted reluctantly. He thought of Major Denton, and his overbearing wife, who had been determined that Conlon would marry their only daughter, Chastity. The woman followed him wherever she could, her loathsome daughter trailing behind. He hadn't had a moment's peace while they were at the camp, and he didn't want to repeat the experience. For Captain Wilton's sake he had been polite, but he didn't know how he had managed.

Captain Wilton interrupted his reverie. "The Dentons are traveling back to Tucson from up north. They will be staying here for a few weeks. I gather Mrs. Denton wants a rest. Also, the major and I need to discuss troop movements and some of the problems with Indians in the area."

"They're staying here?" Conlon glanced at Glorianna. Could Josiah have been right? Was disaster, in the form of Chastity Denton, right around the corner?

eleven

The early morning air caressed her cheek with chilled fingers. Glorianna took a deep breath, savoring the fresh scent of rain-washed earth. The predawn darkness faded, preparing for another gorgeous sunrise.

Glorianna padded out of the fort in eager anticipation of another morning visit with Conlon. Every time they met she found something else to admire about him. Today she wanted to ask him about his family. He always hedged around that question, but for some reason she couldn't let it drop.

Conlon sat with his back to her, head bowed. She hesitated, wondering if he was praying. Most mornings he spent time with the Lord. Maybe she should leave him alone. She considered this, then with a shake of her head she wound through the desert plants toward their rock.

As she drew near, Conlon stood and turned to her. "Good morning, Glory." His mischievous smile set her pulse racing. Blue eyes, brighter than daybreak, held her gaze. She longed to reach up and touch his cheek, to run her fingers through his disobedient hair.

"And how do you know this is a good morning?" She smiled, enjoying his teasing.

"Every day the Lord makes is a good one. You should know that by now." The intense look in his eyes took her breath away. "Besides," he continued, softly, "if the morning starts with seeing you, it has to be good."

The heat of a blush stole up her cheeks and she thought for a moment about returning to the safety of her home. Could she trust herself around this charming man who brought out the best and worst in her?

As if reading her thoughts, Conlon gestured to their rock.

"Come on and sit. The show's about to begin."

She relaxed and settled herself on the rock, trying to ignore the tingle that shot through her as his arm brushed against hers. *This should be a bigger rock,* she thought. But there weren't any other rocks big enough to sit on. She leaned away from him, fighting an inner urge to rest her head on his shoulder.

They watched the changing sky in awed silence. Brilliant colors swept across the gray panorama like a wave washing up on the beach, reaching out with all its might, then slowly ebbing back to the ocean.

Conlon took her hand in his. Her small fingers felt at home engulfed by his large ones. The silence wrapped around them like a familiar cloak, comfortable and warm. Oh, how she wanted to know this man better.

"Conlon?" She tried to keep from getting lost in his morning glory gaze. She wanted to remember her objective. "You know so much about me and my family. Why won't you ever tell me about your family and where you come from?"

A look of pain flitted across his face. It happened so fast, she wondered if she imagined it. He released her hand and bent to scoop up a handful of rocks. He toyed with them as she tried to be patient.

After what seemed an eternity, he looked at her, his expression almost grim. "For years, I never talked about my family and my past. Finally, I did tell Josiah, but only because I had to talk to someone. He's been my friend and encourager in the Lord. He got me through some pretty bad times."

Glorianna swallowed, her mouth suddenly dry as dust. Did she really want to know his past? What if he had done something terrible? Could she forgive him? "If you don't want to tell me, you don't have to." She wanted to grab the words back as soon as they popped out of her mouth. She knew a friend should always be willing to listen.

"No. Josiah tells me it helps to talk about the past and he's usually right."

He rolled one of the small pebbles between his fingers then tossed it at a nearby cactus. The plunk of the rock startled a jackrabbit. The rabbit hopped off, his oversized back legs propelling him forward.

"I grew up in a small town near Chicago. I'm the oldest. I had two younger sisters and a younger brother." He paused to throw another rock. "My parents owned a small dairy herd and supplied milk to the town."

He stopped, staring at the gradually lightening sky. Sighing, he looked down at her and smiled sadly. "You'll have to excuse me. I'm not very good at talking about my past. It's hard."

She nodded. "I understand."

"I always helped Dad with the milk route. We worked hard, but that didn't bother me."

Conlon studied his hands as he spoke. "As a teenager I looked forward to Sundays. We finished our work early, then went to church. But. . ." he shook his head slowly and sighed. "I loved going to church for all the wrong reasons. I liked seeing my friends and being sought after by the girls. I was always the center of attention. The girls and I flirted constantly. To me that was the sole reason for going to church. I never thought about the Lord back then. I was too full of myself."

Conlon's shoulders sagged and Glorianna found herself wanting to wrap him in her arms. She wanted to take away the pain of his past and help him heal.

"I've always had a problem with patience, or I should say, a lack of patience. One Sunday, we were running late on our milk run. My dad was sick, and I had to do most of the work. We barely got home and he collapsed in bed. All I could think about was getting ready for church. Suzanne, one of the cutest girls in town, had promised to sit with me that morning, and I didn't want to miss such an opportunity."

A rock arced out and thudded against another unlucky cactus. "I didn't even help Mom get Dad in bed. All I could think about was me, me, me. Usually, Dad and I got the horse hitched to the wagon so Mom and the girls could ride into town. That morning, my sisters were fighting so they weren't ready yet. My brother, the youngest of the family, wasn't ready, either. Mom called after me, but I acted like I didn't hear her. I jumped on my horse and left for church, soothing my conscience by saying church was more important than family. Besides, I tried to tell myself that my brother, Andy, could get the horse hitched up just fine."

He tossed the rest of the rocks on the ground and wiped his hands on his pants. "I knew better than to do that. We had a new horse, fresh broke and feisty. Andy didn't have much experience with horses yet. He'd been sickly from the time he was born. Small and frail. He couldn't do the same work I had done at his age. I didn't take that into account. Didn't want to. I only wanted to get to church before someone else claimed my seat beside Suzanne."

He sat in silence for so long Glorianna didn't think he would finish his story. His shoulders slumped and the glimpse she had of his blue eyes made her realize they threatened to overflow. Her heart ached for him.

Gently, she placed her hand on his arm. She could feel the muscles knotted beneath his shirt. He looked down at her, and she tried to give him a comforting smile, hoping to relieve his obvious distress.

"We all do things we regret," she spoke up softly. "Especially when we're young and self-centered. Believe me, everyone goes through that at some time." Her words, meant to comfort, had the opposite reaction. His eyes darkened in anger, whether directed at her or himself she didn't know. She fought the urge to back away from him, keeping her hand on his arm.

"You don't understand," he exploded. Closing his eyes, he took a few deep breaths as if trying to calm himself before he continued. "I'm sorry. I didn't mean to get angry." He gave her another sad smile that tore at her heart. "Let me finish, and then maybe you'll see what I mean."

Once more his hand enveloped hers, this time with a feeling

of desperation. "We were halfway through the church service when one of our neighbors burst through the door shouting for Doc Riley. I'd been fighting a growing fear and guilt because my family hadn't shown up yet. I knew how much going to church meant to my mother."

He paused and Glorianna spoke up. "Your father was seriously ill, wasn't he?"

"No, it was Andy who needed the doctor." Conlon cleared his throat. "Andy tried to get the new horse hitched to the wagon. The horse must have sensed his fear and inexperience and began to act up. Andy wanted to please Dad and Mom, I'm sure, so he continued trying. Finally, I guess the horse had enough. He reared up, throwing Andy to the ground. When the horse came down, his hoof hit Andy in the head." Conlon choked and couldn't continue. A solitary tear rolled down his cheek.

Glorianna could feel tears flowing down her cheeks, as well. She gripped Conlon's hand tightly, trying to ease his pain from these horrible memories. "Did Andy. . .?" She didn't know how to ask the question.

"He died two days later." Conlon raked his fingers through his hair. "My oldest sister had started out to help him. She saw what happened, but couldn't get there in time. My dad recovered from his illness, but never from his grief. Even Mom, with her strong faith, had a sadness about her that I couldn't take. I blamed it on my selfishness and impatience."

"Is that why you left home?"

He nodded. "I know they didn't really blame me or if they did, they forgave me, Still, I couldn't live with the blame I put on myself. I ran. Like a coward, I ran and haven't been home since."

"You mean you haven't heard from your parents since you left home?" Glorianna couldn't keep the astonishment from her voice.

Conlon looked at her and shook his head. "For years, they had no idea where I was, so they couldn't write to me."

"Have you thought about writing them now?"

He smiled and squeezed her hand. "When I came here I was angry and confused. Josiah stepped in and helped me find my way to the Lord. Now, I don't attend church because there isn't one, but I have a relationship with the Lord that gives me peace about the past. I wrote to my parents. I apologized for everything that happened and told them where I am and what I'm doing. That was several months ago, and I still haven't heard from them."

"Maybe they've moved. Sometimes letters take awhile to reach people."

"Maybe." He sighed. "Then again, they may just want to forget me."

The sound of a trumpet drifted through the morning air. "I guess that's my call to get back inside. Thanks for listening."

Conlon stood and she let him pull her to her feet. "Thanks for telling me. I know how hard that was for you."

For a long minute, he stood looking down into her eyes. Her heart began to pound and she wondered if he would kiss her. She wondered if she would let him. Then, he leaned over and kissed her lightly on the forehead before tucking her arm in his and heading to the camp.

❧

Josiah gave a final blow to the horseshoe on the anvil, then looked at Conlon, his eyes dancing with merriment. "Why the long face this morning, my friend? Are the wedding plans on hold?"

Conlon shrugged. "They're right on target, I think."

Josiah wiped his hands on his blacksmith apron and studied Conlon for a moment. "Something's wrong," he stated. "You haven't looked this bad since before you asked Jesus into your heart. What happened?"

"I don't know how you do it." Conlon grinned, feeling a peace settling over him. Talking about his past always hurt. He didn't know why being with Josiah helped him so much. "I think God must tell you exactly what I'm thinking and feeling."

Josiah laughed. "Well, someone has to tell me because you sure won't unless I make you."

"I talked to Glorianna this morning." Conlon leaned against the side of the blacksmith shop and watched for Josiah's reaction.

"I thought you talked to her every morning."

"I mean, I talked to her about my family."

Josiah straightened up from throwing wood into the forge. "And?"

"You know, I didn't want to tell her, but now I'm glad I did. She really seemed to understand. She didn't condemn me like I might have done in her place. She's very concerned about my being in touch with my family."

"I knew that girl had something special." Josiah's grin lit up his face. He laughed. "You'd better get her to marry you quick or some other lucky man will get her first."

"Not a chance. I won't let them get close."

"By the way, I heard the captain's looking for you. Maybe he wants to know when you're setting the date." Josiah laughed.

Conlon strode toward the captain's office. With every passing minute he felt better about having talked to Glorianna. He hadn't wanted to hold anything back from her and now he knew nothing stood between them. Perhaps Josiah spoke the truth. He should talk to the captain and his daughter about a wedding. He smiled as he thought of finally being able to hold Glory in his arms without letting her go.

He stepped into the captain's office and stood at attention, waiting for him to look up from the papers on his desk. The early morning sounds of the camp blurred into a drone through the thick walls. Finally, Captain Wilton looked up, his face set in a frown. Conlon felt the first prick of uncertainty. What did he want?

"Lieutenant." Captain Wilton's booming voice almost startled him. "I'm afraid we have a little problem. I received word that some Apaches are making trouble over toward

Pinal City. They were last reported heading into the Superstition Mountains. I want you to take some men and check it out."

Conlon stood frozen, wanting to protest, knowing it wouldn't be wise. *But, I want to stay here with your daughter,* he wanted to say. *I don't want to miss my morning talks with her.* Despite all his protesting thoughts he replied, "Yes, Sir."

With a heavy heart he spent the rest of the morning looking over maps and making plans with the captain. He tried hard to forget his red-haired beauty and the Sonoran sunrise they loved to share.

twelve

Conlon leaned back against his saddle, his long frame stretched close to the campfire. Millions of stars paraded across the dark sky like tiny twinkling fireflies. The sounds of the desert descended upon him, the high-pitched yips of a pack of coyotes cut short by the unearthly scream of a cougar. Good thing he had posted guards around the camp.

He rolled to his side and stared at the fire. For two weeks, he and his small troop of men had searched the Superstition Mountains for the band of Apaches reported to be terrorizing the countryside. Each moment of the two weeks had been sheer torture. Every day he thought only of getting back to Glorianna, seeing her bright smile and talking with her in the mornings. How he longed to run his fingers over her smooth cheeks. He wanted to watch the rose blush travel over her apple blossom complexion like the sunrise traveled across the sky. Glorianna. How he missed her.

He knew the men thought him totally inept. He kept running them in circles, forgetting the direction from which they had come. Thank God, Timothy had been assigned to the group. Without his encouragement, Conlon would have given up days ago. Timothy understood how hard leading could be when you had a woman on your mind.

Another week, he thought. *I'll give this scouting expedition one more week. If we don't see more than some old tracks we'll head back to Camp MacDowell. There's no need to wear ourselves out when the Indians have already moved on to other parts. They're probably miles from here laughing at how easily they fooled us. We've never even gotten a glimpse of them. Of course, it doesn't help when we don't get word about them until they've had a week's head start.*

He shifted on his bedroll, hoping the hard ground would get softer. *You'd think after two weeks I'd be used to sleeping on the ground. But, then, after two weeks I should be over thinking about Glory all the time, too.* A sudden longing made him grit his teeth in frustration. He could almost feel his arms around her. He could see her rosebud mouth smiling up at him. How would it feel to press his lips to hers? To run his fingers through her silken hair? To hear her say, "I love you"? Smiling, he drifted off to sleep as the coyotes, once again, began their nightly chorus.

Morning dawned, bright and clear. Conlon hurried the men through their breakfast, determined they would find some sign or direction today. As soon as these Indians were controlled, he could return to Camp MacDowell and Glory. The very thought of seeing her made him smile.

Four hours later, hot and discouraged, his small troop rested in the shade of a side canyon. They had followed old hoof prints along the side of the canyon, hoping to find a place where the Indians had hidden. It turned out to be a dead end. The only way out was a steep cliff that a horse could never climb.

"Where to, Lieutenant?" Timothy crouched next to Conlon.

"I guess we'll head toward the north end of the mountains. It's closest to Pinal City, and we haven't gone all the way around yet."

Timothy squinted up at the sun. "I wish there weren't so many places to hide in these mountains. You know, they come here because of that. They can disappear without a trace, wait for us to give up, then continue their raids whenever they want."

"I know," Conlon agreed. "I wish I knew a better way. We don't have the knowledge of the land like the Indians do. They can survive on almost nothing and hide behind the smallest bush."

Conlon stood and stared off into the empty desert. "Let's go, men." They mounted and headed back into the open. The intense heat seemed to suck the life out of them one step at a time.

"Lieutenant." Timothy shaded his eyes, staring ahead. "There's a dust cloud ahead. Riders are circling the mountains."

"Fall into formation, men," Conlon directed. "Let's ride."

Even the horses seemed to sense the excitement of the moment. They lifted their heads and rolled into a canter, manes and tails streaming in the wind. Maybe this would end their search. Maybe this was their long-sought quarry.

For long minutes they kept up the pace. Then, the distant dust cloud drifted away. Conlon slowed the column to a trot, wondering if, once again, the Indians had simply disappeared without a trace. Had they imagined the horses ahead? What if the desert heat and the desire to fulfill their mission made the whole company see a mirage? He shook his head. The very idea was ridiculous.

Topping a rise, Conlon raised his hand, calling a halt. Below them a group of horses and riders gathered close. They were so intent on each other they obviously didn't see the small group of soldiers above them. The riders' saddles creaked. Sunlight glinted off their gun barrels. The yellow stripes on their pant legs caught the eye. These weren't Indians. They were cavalrymen.

Conlon allowed Champ to pick his way down the slope. As small rocks skittered down the hill ahead of them, the men stopped their conference and looked up. Conlon counted a dozen, some in uniform, some in regular clothes. As he and his men approached, the soldiers pulled back, leaving two older men to face them. Clearly, they were in charge.

For a moment, he studied the two men. The one on the right had a commanding air about him. He didn't wear a uniform, but his bearing conveyed the message of his military position. Only an officer of rank could do that with such ease.

The second officer looked vaguely familiar. His grim face sported a huge mustache that covered his mouth and dripped well past his chin. Bushy eyebrows drew together in a frown as he studied Conlon.

"Lieutenant Sullivan, Camp MacDowell, Sir." Conlon held himself erect, watching the reaction of the two men.

"Sullivan?" The heavy mustache opened to release the words. "Are you the Sullivan serving under Captain Wilton?"

That voice tickled a memory somewhere. Conlon nodded. "Yes, Sir."

The mustache split in a grin, a deep chuckle issuing forth to break the man's angry countenance. "I guess you don't remember me, Son."

Son? Who was this man to call him son?

The man continued. "I'm Major Denton."

"Yes, Sir, I remember." *And want to forget,* he thought. "I believe Captain Wilton is expecting your family to visit Camp MacDowell."

"That's right." The big man frowned. "We've had a slight delay, but we plan to get there soon." He gestured to the man on the horse next to him. "You've probably heard of General Crook. General, this young lieutenant took quite a liking to my daughter. He's the reason she's so anxious to return to Camp MacDowell." A hearty laugh followed.

General Crook's gaze hadn't faltered or changed visibly, but Conlon felt the intensity increase just the same. *Took a liking to his daughter?* Conlon wanted to groan in frustration, but kept his expression neutral, pasting a smile on his face.

"Pleasure to meet you, General. I've heard a lot about your campaigns from Arizona Territory to Montana." Conlon had long admired General George Crook and his expertise in tracking and fighting the Indians. He was a legend among the cavalry.

"You know, General," Major Denton said, "Lieutenant Sullivan may be the answer to our problem."

At Crook's nod, Major Denton turned back to Conlon. "We're camped a few miles from here. We were on our way to Camp MacDowell when the general found us. I agreed to help him round up the Apaches who are causing trouble, but we didn't know what to do with my wife and daughter."

Forcing himself to stay calm, Conlon didn't want to hear what the major was thinking. *Please, God, don't let him ask me what I think he wants to ask.*

"Why don't you and your men escort them to Camp MacDowell. Then, we can use all our men and really get after these Indians."

"I'd love to help you out, Sir, but Captain Wilton sent us on a mission to find the marauders. I don't think he would want me to quit before we had tried everything we could to catch them."

"Nonsense." The bushy eyebrows drew together in another frown. "The general and I are superior officers here. If we give you a different set of orders, your captain can't possibly object. Besides, I'll be at the camp as soon as I can and settle the matter."

"We'll send you written orders, Lieutenant," General Crook said. "The ladies need to be someplace other than a rough camp in the desert."

Conlon ordered his men to fall in line for the trip to the major's camp. *God, please give me the patience for this,* he pleaded. *If Mrs. Denton and Chastity are as bad as before, I may be tempted to leave them for coyote bait in the desert.*

Then again, he smiled ruefully, *what do I have against the coyotes?*

ta

"Lieutenant Conlon Sullivan." The high-pitched squeal made Conlon groan all the way down to his toes. Chastity stood before him, batting her blue eyes and fluffing her blond curls, trying her best to look coy. Her attempts failed.

"Hello, Miss Denton."

"Oh, none of this 'Miss Denton' business." She dipped her parasol and smiled impishly. "We know each other too well for such formality. Just call me Chastity." She placed her hand on his arm possessively.

He felt like his face would probably rival the deep pink sky of the sunrise. *God, I can't take Chastity to Camp MacDowell with me. What will Glorianna think? The two of them will be like cats with their tails tied together.* He groaned inwardly, thinking of Josiah's warning of impending doom.

さ

Dearest Kathleen,

I can't thank you enough for writing to me about Kendrick. I don't know why I was so blinded by his charms. I believe he always represented adventure to me. All the other girls were wild about him, and I followed along for some unknown reason. Actually, I guess the reason was pretty obvious. I wanted to fit in.

Because of Mother's illness and our travels as I grew up, I didn't have many friends. You are my only friend there and, believe me, you were enough. I thank you for standing by me even when my thickheaded ways threatened to undo me.

I do have a friend here. I wish you could come out and meet Fayth. She's older than I am and married. She has the sweetest little girl, Alyce. If we didn't live in such a remote area, I would invite you to come out here. Maybe some day I will anyway.

Glorianna stopped and chewed thoughtfully on the end of her pen. Kathleen, sweet and steady, always confided her longing for marriage and a family. Unfortunately, a birthmark splashed across her cheek marred her looks. Despite her deep faith in God and His purpose for her life, Kathleen grieved because none of the eligible young men would notice her. Glorianna frowned; at least they didn't notice her positively. They constantly made hateful remarks and tormented her because of her looks. Not one of the louts took the time to see Kathleen's inner beauty.

As I am writing, I remember Father saying he expects

*to get a transfer this fall. Maybe we'll go someplace near
a city and you could join us. Being in a camp like Mac-
Dowell is a little lonely, but I'm told there are some nice
cities in Arizona Territory. Maybe we'll even go to Fort
Lowell just outside of Tucson. I've heard it's a nice town.*

She stopped writing again, thinking how to word the next
part of her letter. Laughing blue eyes danced across her
vision. How she missed Conlon. For a few mornings she
continued to go to their rock and watch the sunrise. It wasn't
the same with Conlon gone. The colors seemed pale without
him there to talk to. She couldn't wait for him to get back.

*You were right about something else, Kathleen. There
are other men. I've finally realized that. In fact, I've met a
man I feel is right for me. Fayth recommended the same
thing you always did. She said I should look for godly
attributes in a man. Conlon Sullivan is just that—a godly
man.*

*We've been meeting in the mornings to watch the sun-
rise. Conlon always gets up to have a time alone with
God. I happened to find out and began to join him. Now,
if I don't see him early, my day isn't the same. Right now
he's off with some men tracking down renegade Indians.
I can't tell you how much I miss his presence. I do wish
you could meet him. I know you would love him, too.*

She could just picture Conlon and Kathleen together. He
wouldn't even notice her birthmark, or if he did he would
only comment on how the star-shaped mark enhanced her
beauty. And they wouldn't be empty words, either. Conlon
cared about people and saw beauty where others didn't. As
she thought, the conviction grew that she needed to bring
Kathleen out west to help her heal from life's hurts.

A knock at the door interrupted Glorianna. She carefully
put the pen in the inkwell and hurried to answer. Fayth and

Alyce beamed at her from the front step.

"Come in. I'm glad you dropped by." She laughed. "I'm so bored I'm actually writing a letter to my cousin. She'll be shocked to hear from me so soon. I'm terrible with letters."

Fayth's eyes twinkled. "I have some news for you."

"What?" Glorianna held her breath, hoping this was the news she wanted to hear.

"They've been spotted. The men will be here in about half an hour."

Alyce clapped her hands, then held them out to Glorianna. "Daddy, home."

Glorianna swung the girl up in the air. "You're right. Daddy's home, Sweetheart. I'll bet you'll be glad to see him."

"I'll bet you'll be glad to see someone, too." Fayth's knowing gaze sent heat creeping up Glorianna's cheeks.

"I couldn't possibly know what you mean." Glorianna tilted her head and fluffed her hair. Then she dissolved in giggles and kissed Alyce on the cheek. "I can't wait to see him. It seems like forever."

Later, at the mercantile, Glorianna dropped off the letter she'd written to Kathleen then hurried to follow Fayth across the parade ground. The milling horses and men told them the troop had returned. Her heart raced as she searched the crowd for Conlon's familiar face. She couldn't wait to see him.

"Oh, dear." Fayth's soft whisper barely reached her ears.

She turned to look in the direction Fayth was looking. Conlon stood at the side of a wagon, reaching up to help a young woman down. He swung her easily to the ground. She wrapped her arms around his, leaned on him, and smiled up at him.

Melissa? Glorianna couldn't believe it. How could Melissa Cornwall have come here? The slim form and the blond curls looked just like Melissa's. First Kendrick and now Conlon. Would she never be rid of her rival? Her insides began a slow burn, gradually building in intensity as she watched that brazen female ooze all over Conlon.

thirteen

Conlon remembered, years before, falling in the muck of the pigpen after a good rain. The slimy goo stuck to his clothes, his skin, his hair, and everywhere. He thought he would never get it washed off. Chastity Denton reminded him of that slimy goo. She clung to his arm like a leech, a leech he feared he might never dislodge.

Tugging his arm in an attempt to at least loosen her grip, he glanced up to see disaster heading his way. A red-haired, green-eyed ball of fury rolled across the ground on a collision course with him. Desperately, he searched for a way of escape. From the other direction the ultimate catastrophe approached. Like a ship parting the waters of the ocean, Mrs. Denton sailed through the milling soldiers toward them. *God, don't leave me stranded here,* he begged, hating the helplessness of the situation.

"Lieutenant Sullivan." Sounding like a train making an emergency stop, Mrs. Denton had everyone's attention. Conlon winced and tried to turn away, moving his shoulder perilously close to Chastity's head. She took advantage of the situation by leaning against him and rubbing her cheek on his arm. He gritted his teeth and groaned.

"What is going on here?" Glorianna's normally melodic voice could cut through solid rock. Conlon watched helplessly as her green eyes flashed a fire that pierced his heart. He begged her with his eyes, hoping she'd understand his dilemma, but his silent plea didn't seem to help.

Taking a deep breath, Conlon knew he had to do something to redeem the situation. Sending up a silent prayer, he made one more unsuccessful attempt to dislodge Chastity before speaking.

"Excuse me, ladies." For the moment he had their attention. "Glorianna, I'd like you to meet Mrs. Denton and her daughter, Chastity." He tried to move his arm in a gesture, but the leech clung to him. "Mrs. Denton, Chastity, please meet Glorianna Wilton, Captain Wilton's daughter."

The three women eyed each other like vultures prepared to fight over their prey. To his relief, some of the fire faded from Glorianna's eyes as she studied Chastity.

"I'm pleased to meet you ladies." Although softer, her tone still had an edge.

Mrs. Denton sniffed, looked Glorianna up and down, and then nodded in her direction in obvious dismissal. The insult fanned the flames of fury and the green eyes flashed fire again.

Chastity followed her mother's example. Lifting her nose in the air, she once more began to rub against Conlon's arm like a cat begging for attention.

"Lieutenant Sullivan," Mrs. Denton spoke sharply, "you will show us to our quarters. I believe the captain's quarters will suffice. They were pleasant enough when we were here last."

From the corner of his eye, Conlon watched Glorianna's jaw drop. "I'm sorry, Ma'am." He talked fast, hoping to calm the threatening storm. "The captain and his daughter are there. I'm sure our guest quarters will be fine."

Mrs. Denton, no doubt unaccustomed to having her orders questioned, began to resemble a lobster tossed in a kettle of boiling water. "We will stay in the captain's quarters, Lieutenant." Her tone brooked no discussion. "The captain and his daughter can stay in the guest quarters if they wish."

"What?" Oh, no, Glorianna had finally found her voice.

"Mrs. Denton. Chastity."

Conlon almost cried in relief as Fayth stepped forward, a smile lighting her face. "It's so good to have you visit us again."

Mrs. Denton stared hard at Fayth, whose smile never wavered. "Oh, yes, I remember you. Your husband is one of lower rank." The condescending tone and pointed insult made Conlon wince.

"I'm Fayth Holwell. We heard you were planning to join us. The guest quarters have been freshened and cleaned just for you."

"You forget, Mrs. Holwell, I've seen your guest quarters. We will stay in the captain's house as we did before." Mrs. Denton's features softened as she looked at her daughter. "Besides, Chastity needs a room of her own rather than a front room everyone tramps through."

Glorianna stepped up to Mrs. Denton looking undaunted. The larger woman towered over her. "My father and I are using his quarters, Mrs. Denton." Glorianna's slow, deliberate speech betrayed her anger. "You and your daughter may stay in the guest quarters like any other visitors to Camp MacDowell."

The two combatants faced one another in silence for what seemed an eternity. Mrs. Denton pulled herself up to her full height and turned from Glorianna.

"We'll see about this. Come, Chastity, I'm going to talk to the captain." With that she sailed off through the crowd.

Chastity unwound herself from Conlon and followed her mother with hesitant steps. She turned back for a moment and smiled coyly at Conlon, her ice blue eyes freezing his blood. "I'll be back." Her sultry tones nearly set the ground on fire. "We can take up where we left off then." She turned and sashayed after her mother.

Glorianna swung around and faced him.

God, Conlon prayed, *this would be a good time for an earthquake. Let the ground just open up and swallow me. Or maybe an Indian arrow between the shoulder blades would be nice. Anything but what I'm facing, Lord. I do believe I might be a little cowardly in this instance.*

Glorianna's mouth opened and he winced, waiting for the diatribe. Her mouth closed again without having issued a sound.

She's speechless! Lord, I didn't know You could do miracles like this. Thank You.

"Glory, I know you're angry, but please let me explain."

Fayth stepped up beside Glorianna, her arms crossed over her chest.

Oh, Lord, not Fayth, too.

"Glory, Chastity and her mother determined the last time they were here that I would make a perfect husband for Chastity." He swallowed hard, trying not to shudder at the memory. "I've never encouraged her. I don't want to marry her. I don't even like her."

Did he detect some softening in both women? Taking a deep breath, he continued, "Please believe me, she means nothing to me."

"Then why was she draped all over you like a winter coat?" Glorianna's voice could still cut iron.

"Because I can't seem to convince her that I'm not good husband material." Desperation began to set in. "I don't know what to do to change her opinion of me. Once Mrs. Denton and Chastity decide something, they never change their minds."

Fayth's sudden smile felt like the sun after a rainy day. "He's right. Mrs. Denton runs her own household like a general and assumes she can run the rest of the world, too." She sighed. "I don't mean to speak ill of the woman, but her last visit was far from pleasant. She had the whole camp in an uproar by the time she left."

Conlon couldn't take his eyes off Glorianna's lips. They were lifting into a smile, a sight he thought he'd never see again. He could only think about how those lips would feel meeting his own. A sudden longing to hold her close almost overwhelmed him.

"I understand a little better." Glorianna smiled. "Just think about the desert heat and remember you don't need a winter coat."

"I'll do that." Relief flooded through him. "Now, if you ladies will excuse me, I need to see to the men." He started to turn away, then wheeled back around to Glorianna. Taking her hand in his, he ran his thumb over the soft skin. "I can't wait to see the sunrise tomorrow."

❧

That afternoon, Glorianna gritted her teeth and stared in stony silence at the desert rolling by the ambulance. They were heading for the Verde River for their evening time to bathe and cool off. She knew she needed more than a river to help her cool off. The heat of anger had been building all day, ever since she first saw Chastity Denton and her mother.

Sighing, she recalled the talk she and Fayth had earlier that afternoon.

"Glorianna, you have to realize that Conlon is a cavalry-man. It's his duty to follow orders and please his superiors. If that means escorting a beautiful girl around then that's what he has to do. It doesn't mean he likes it."

"But, I hate the way she leans on him and smiles up at him. She acts like she owns him." Glorianna detested the whine in her voice.

"You know Conlon is not interested in her. It only takes one look at his face to see he's miserable around her."

"I suppose you're right."

"I am right. Conlon only has eyes for one beautiful girl and that's you."

"So what should I do?"

"Try to remember what a good Christian should do. You love her and treat her like you want to be treated." Fayth reached out and gave her a quick hug. *"I know that's far easier to say than to do. With God's help you can, though."*

"I'll try." Glorianna promised.

❧

Of course, that promise was made before she knew the extent of Mrs. Denton's formidable power. She soon learned that even her father quailed before the enemy. She knew he felt he made concessions, but it didn't help her at all. He finally decided that he would sleep in the officers' quarters. Mrs. Denton and the major, when he arrived, would have her

father's room. The worst part was that he expected her to
share her room with Chastity. That would be like crawling
into bed every night with a rattlesnake or, even worse, a
viper.

To her credit, Chastity hadn't been happy about the situation, either. She whined and pleaded to no avail. Chastity
knew when she pushed as far as she could. Since then, she
had done her best to irritate Glorianna at every turn.

The wagon pulled to a stop and the women began to climb
down. The men tied their horses and hurried to help before
they continued down the river to their spot. Glorianna watched
Chastity, sitting with her parasol twirling over her head, her
blue eyes fastened on Conlon.

"Lieutenant." The sultry tone made Glorianna nauseous.
"Help me down." Chastity cocked her head to one side and
held out her hands, batting her blue eyes. Her ruby lips pursed
in a sensual smile.

She could be Melissa's twin, Glorianna thought. *She has
the same eyes, the same hair, the same coquettish attitude,
and probably the same low standards judging from the way
she plastered herself to him earlier.*

Conlon approached the wagon, his jaw muscles tense,
his eyes dark and narrowed. He did not look pleased with
Chastity. He reached up, grasped her small waist, and fairly
threw her to the ground. She barely caught her balance when
he circled away from her to the front of the ambulance where
Glorianna sat.

He stopped beside her and Glorianna could see his struggle to control his anger. "May I help you down, Glory?" he
asked softly. His words carried in the silence as the whole
group watched the exchange.

"Thank you, Conlon." Glorianna tried to make her smile
especially bright for him. The next moment his hands were circling her waist. Wrapping her fingers around his arms, she felt
the tensing of his muscles as he lifted her effortlessly over the
side of the wagon. He gently deposited her on the ground in

front of him, holding her longer than necessary. For a moment she thought he might kiss her. Instead, he ran one finger down her cheek, smiled, winked, and stepped back.

She glanced at Chastity, gratified to see her red face and angry stance. Mrs. Denton stood near her daughter, doing an amazing resemblance of a thundercloud during a summer rainstorm. "Come, Chastity." Mrs. Denton's voice grated in the silence. "Let's not watch such a tawdry display."

Glorianna noticed Fayth and Timothy turning away, trying to hide their smiles. Several of the others chuckled quietly. Activity resumed. The men headed down the path to their part of the river. Glorianna followed Fayth and Alyce down the slope of the riverbank hoping she could control her dislike of Chastity and her mother.

Awhile later, Alyce laughed with glee as she watched Glorianna spurt water in the air by pushing it up through her hands. Alyce loved water games, splashing her chubby hands and squealing when the water sprayed her face. She made a dive for her mother, going under the water before she reached her. Fayth pulled her up, shaking her head as Alyce sprayed them with water while she spluttered and laughed.

"Alyce, I don't think my heart can stand more of this." Fayth shook her head. "You have no fear of this water. I think it's time to get out."

Glorianna laughed and watched the pair head for the bank. She didn't notice who moved up beside her until Chastity spoke in her ear. The sultry tones had changed, sounding like a lower-pitched version of Mrs. Denton.

"So, you think Lieutenant Sullivan is going to be yours. I just want you to know you're wrong," Chastity said.

Glorianna reluctantly swung around. Ice blue eyes bored into her.

"He's mine," Chastity hissed. "My mother promised me I'd marry him, and she always gets what she wants."

"I believe Lieutenant Sullivan can choose a wife for himself." Glorianna tried hard to push her anger down.

"Oh, but you're wrong there." Chastity's smile could freeze fire. "He's a military man. My father has a lot of rank on him. Lieutenant Sullivan will have to do what he's told."

"Marriage is a little different than following orders on a parade ground."

"My father can make his life miserable. Is that what you want for your precious lieutenant? If you really feel something for him, you'll give up now."

Chastity's smirk proved too much.

"If you excuse me, I believe I'll join Fayth and Alyce at the wagon." Glorianna stood. She started to take a step, then wobbled. Her arms windmilled. In a flash, she fell on top of Chastity, pushing her beneath the rippling water of the Verde River.

Chastity pushed back and Glorianna leaned harder on her, acting like she couldn't get her balance. The other women began to rush toward her. Just before they reached her she sat back. Chastity broke the surface, gulping in air, looking like a drowned rat. Her blond curls, now limp, hung in a tangled mass.

"Do forgive me," Glorianna purred. "These rocks can be tricky. I must have slipped on one." With that, she rose and, as gracefully as possible, left the river.

fourteen

Glorianna leaned against the house, rubbing her arms against the early morning chill. Stars still twinkled overhead, their light not yet dimmed by the approaching dawn. A dove's haunting cry echoed over the chirp of crickets. In the distance a lone coyote howled a message about the night's hunt.

Her eyes burned. She fought against the tightening in her throat and chest. She hated crying. She wouldn't give in to tears over some flirtatious fool like Chastity Denton. A lone teardrop traced a wet, cool path down her cheek.

"What am I to do?" Glorianna whispered to the night. "I'm going crazy staying in a room with her." For the last three weeks, she had shared her room with Chastity while Mrs. Denton took over the rest of the house, running it like some sort of queen. She told Glorianna what to wear, how to act, and where she could go.

Visiting Fayth hadn't been high on the list of things Mrs. Denton encouraged, either. *After all,* Glorianna could hear her say, *your father is a captain and you have certain standards to which you must measure up. You must watch whom you befriend.*

Well, her mother hadn't felt that way. She loved everyone, welcoming anyone into her house. But, her mother also taught her to respect her elders. Glorianna determined not to disappoint her mother or her father.

The hardest part of the last few weeks had to do with Conlon. They hadn't had a minute alone. Mrs. Denton insisted he escort Chastity everywhere. His only break came when he had military duties to perform. Even some of those were given to the other men so he could be at the Dentons' beck and call.

Oh, she knew he didn't enjoy the duty. Having to be attentive to Chastity's every whim was taking its toll. Dark shadows ringed Conlon's eyes. His face seemed drawn and haggard. His blue eyes rarely held their merry twinkle. At least, when she got close enough to him to see his eyes. Chastity made sure he and Glorianna kept their distance.

"Mother, I wish you were here." Glorianna's whispered words echoed the ache in her heart. "Daddy is letting this woman run over the top of him. I know you would have been able to set things right. You were always good at settling disputes among the ladies everywhere we went. Now, I don't know where to turn."

Tears ran down her cheeks. She bit her lip to stifle a sob. She didn't want to wake Mrs. Denton or Chastity. She didn't want them to know she'd slipped out early to be by herself. Today, for the first time since they had arrived, she had managed to get out of the house without Mrs. Denton's waking and demanding to know where she was going before daylight.

Glorianna pushed away from the house. She hoped Conlon would be at their rock today. Maybe, just maybe, they could have a few minutes together. She crossed the parade ground, going first to the stables. Despite the dark, she knew the way well enough. The sound of an occasional stomping foot thudded against the floor. She had to see Nina. Even her horse had been forced to desert her. Chastity demanded the right to ride her and had, of course, gotten her way.

"Hey, Sweetie." Glorianna stroked the satiny muzzle. Nina nickered and blew against her hand. "I'm sorry I don't have a treat for you. It was too risky to go in the kitchen for a sugar lump. I'll try to bring one later."

She wrapped her arms around Nina's neck. "Sometimes I want to get on you and ride away from here." She breathed deeply, drawing comfort from the horse's earthy scent. "I can't do it, though. I've fallen in love with Conlon, and I can't leave him behind." The horse's thick neck muffled her sobs of despair.

&

Conlon dropped down on the rock. He rubbed his face with his hands, then swept his hair back from his forehead. *God, I'm sorry I've been so lax in my meetings with You lately. Those women are making me crazy. Mrs. Denton is sure I'm the perfect husband for Chastity. She doesn't even care what I think of the idea. All I've done these last few weeks is pamper a spoiled child—for that's exactly what Chastity is.*

The skittering sound of a night animal running for shelter interrupted his thoughts. He watched the sky for a moment, knowing that before long it would begin to lighten in preparation for another day. *Another day wasted,* he thought. His mouth twisted into a grimace of disgust. How could he manage to be polite to Chastity and her mother? How much more could he take before he really exploded?

What he wanted to do was spend the day with Glorianna. How he missed their mornings together. He missed her lilting laugh. He wanted to touch her, talk to her, tell her how much he loved her. A groan escaped as he thought of the sweet scent of roses that belonged to Glory. *God, what am I to do? How long must I wait?*

He hadn't slept well lately. Thoughts of Glory and Chastity fought a war in his head every night. How could he resolve this dilemma? *I guess the truth is, I can't do a thing, Lord. Once more, I have to leave this in Your hands.*

Memories of the previous night drifted before his eyes. Chastity, always too forward, nearly threw herself at him when her mother wasn't looking. Mrs. Denton kept prattling on about his speaking with the major when he arrived tomorrow. She expected him to ask for her daughter's hand in marriage when, in truth, he couldn't stand the thought of even touching Chastity's hand.

Late last night, by the light of a candle, he searched his Bible, looking for some word from God. Psalm 37:7 kept coming to him over and over. "Rest in the Lord, and wait patiently for him. . . ." Conlon shook his head, wondering again how long the Lord expected him to be patient and wait.

Recalling long rides and even longer walks with Chastity made his stomach turn. He couldn't stand the way she flaunted herself. Always one to get her way, she expected him to put her first in everything they did. She never gave a thought to anyone else's feelings.

The scrape of a shoe on the sandy desert startled him. *Oh, God, please don't let Chastity have found me so early,* he groaned. Pushing himself up from the rock, he turned to face the intruder. To his surprise, it wasn't Chastity or her mother coming to begin their daily torments.

"Glory!" He longed to rush to her and scoop her up in his arms. Something held him back. He gestured to the rock. "Come and join me. We have a little time to talk before the sunrise."

"I'd like that." Glorianna's smile warmed him. "We haven't had many chances to see each other these past few weeks."

He waited until she made herself comfortable, then he allowed himself the luxury of sitting next to her. He inhaled, closing his eyes for a moment to enjoy the clean, rose scent that drifted to him. He wanted to pull her close, to bury his face in her soft hair, but he mentally shook himself in order to maintain control.

"I haven't been able to get away from Mrs. Denton long enough to come out and watch the sunrise." She looked so forlorn it broke his heart. "I miss our morning talks."

He nodded. "I miss them, too. I've had some trouble getting here of a morning myself. I know God understands. I still have a short time with Him at night, but nothing is quite like these early morning meetings."

"You look tired, Conlon. Are you all right?"

"I'm fine." He tried to smile. "I am a little tired of having my schedule directed by someone other than your father."

Glorianna laughed a dry, humorless laugh. "I think the whole camp is tired of being run by Mrs. Denton. I want to blame Daddy, but I know he tries. Despite his best efforts, she has taken over."

He grinned. "I wonder what will happen when the major shows up tomorrow?"

"Does she run him like she does everyone else?"

"She sure does. I remember the last time they were at the camp; she had everything turned upside down. I don't know how one woman can cause so much disorder in so many lives."

"Conlon." Glorianna's voice barely reached his ears. "I don't know how much longer I can take her interference before I explode. I've tried to be nice, but I'd really rather take her out and tie her to a cactus."

"That would be interesting." Conlon chuckled.

"I can't stand spending another night with Chastity. All she talks about is you."

"And what does she tells you about me?"

She shrugged, silent for a moment. "She talks about how much you love her, about how you plan to ask for her hand in marriage when her father gets here, and how wonderful you will be as a husband."

Conlon watched Glorianna as she talked, hope filling his heart. Was she jealous? Just then the sky overhead burst into color. Conlon barely noticed as he stared at Glorianna, drinking in her beauty.

"Glory, I don't plan to be her husband." He tried to speak firmly, to wash away the despair he thought he could see in her eyes.

"But, she says you're in the cavalry and you have to do what her father says. He's a higher rank."

He couldn't help it; the laughter just bubbled up from deep inside. She was jealous. He understood now. The only way she could be this worried about Chastity was if she truly cared about him.

"In a way she's right." Conlon tried to calm the thundering of his heart. "I do have to obey my superior officers. But that only pertains to military matters. My personal life is my own."

"I know Major Denton can't order you to marry his

daughter, but she says he'll make your life miserable if you don't marry her."

He watched the colors fade from the sky, trying to think of the best way to answer her. He took her small hand in his, running his thumb over her soft skin. "Glory, look at me." He waited until her tear-filled green eyes looked into his. "There is no way Major Denton could make me more miserable than I would be if I married his daughter. I can't think of anything worse."

Her emerald gaze held his for a long time. Slowly, he became aware of the pressure of her fingers as they gripped his. He smiled and almost laughed with joy as an answering smile lit her face.

"Tell me, Glory." He pulled her close, tucking her arm against his side. "What do you want most?"

For a long time she looked lost in thought, then she turned to him. "I used to think all I wanted was a little cottage. I wanted a white picket fence and a flower garden where my friends could come and visit with me." Her eyes took on a dreamy look. "I pictured sitting there with my children, watching them play and laugh."

A look of sadness washed over her face. He longed to touch her and wipe the look away. "What happened to that dream?" he asked.

She took a deep breath and released it slowly. "I just realized something was missing."

"What's that?"

A faint blush stained her creamy cheeks. "You'll think this is silly, but I always dreamed of friends and children. I never had a husband at my cottage."

"Not even Kendrick?"

"Not even him," she spoke thoughtfully. "I see now it was a shallow wish, only for me."

"So what is your dream now?" He held his breath, not daring to hope.

She pursed her lips and tilted her head to one side, looking up at him. "I don't think the cottage and white picket fence matter anymore. I'm sure I'll have friends wherever I go." She paused, then lowered her eyes before continuing. "I guess what matters most to me now is finding the right husband."

His heart raced. He wanted to grab her up and kiss her. He wanted to waltz her around the cactus. *God, please don't let me be impatient here. Help me to have the right words for Glorianna.*

Conlon opened his mouth to speak, but the words wouldn't come. Glorianna looked up and for a long minute he lost himself in her eyes. He reached up and wrapped a strand of her silky hair around his fingers. The burnished red gleamed in the first rays of sunlight.

He tried again. "How will you know when you've found the right husband?" His voice sounded raspy with emotion. He held his breath, waiting for what seemed an eternity for her answer.

Glorianna pulled her hand free from his, leaving his fingers empty. She reached slowly up and softly brushed a stray lock of hair back from his forehead. "I'll know," she whispered. He gasped at the feelings that raced through him. Oh, how he loved this woman.

Releasing her hair, Conlon traced his fingers down her cheek. He remembered doing this once before, but she hadn't been aware of him then. Now, she watched him with wide green eyes. She didn't pull away. In fact, she leaned closer.

Ever so slowly, he lowered his face to hers. His eyes took in the dusting of freckles on her creamy skin. Her scent pulled him closer with rose perfumed fingers. His lips met hers. He wanted the moment to last forever. He slipped his arm around her slender waist.

"I see you were right, Chastity." The harsh, grating voice interrupted their moment. Glorianna pulled back, her face turning pink. Mrs. Denton, with Chastity peeking from behind her, stood like an avenging judge. Her hands on her hips, she glared at Glorianna.

fifteen

"I will have a talk with your father, young lady. You are nothing but a seductress trying to take away my daughter's future husband."

Glorianna flushed a deep red and leaped from the rock. Her foot slipped, and Conlon reached out a hand to steady her. He, too, stood and faced their accusers. Keeping a light hold on Glory's arm, he could feel her tremble.

A sudden anger swept through Conlon as the weight of Mrs. Denton's accusation sank in. "You have no right to judge Glorianna's actions." Clenching his jaw to keep from yelling, his words came out soft, spoken with a deadly calm. "She's done nothing wrong."

Mrs. Denton narrowed her piglike eyes even further and leaned forward. "She knows you and Chastity will be getting married. She has no right to be sneaking around, meeting you in the middle of the night like this."

Glorianna tensed. "This is not the middle of the night, and I did not sneak around."

"Did you tell anyone where you were going?" Mrs. Denton folded her arms across her ample bosom.

"I don't have to tell anyone where I'm going." Glorianna spat out the words. "My father trusts me. I don't fawn all over men like a cheap girl would."

Mrs. Denton's mouth fell open. Her face flushed a cherry red.

"I have not asked for Chastity's hand in marriage." Conlon tried to diffuse the situation. "Nor do I intend to, Mrs. Denton."

"Mama." Chastity began to sob.

"Be quiet, Chastity." Mrs. Denton took a few steps toward Conlon and Glorianna. "Lieutenant, the major will be arriving tomorrow. He will talk to you about this matter. Chastity has counted on your asking for her hand since we were here the last time. You will not disappoint my daughter. Not over a woman like that." She gestured toward Glorianna.

"Now, you," Mrs. Denton lashed out at Glorianna, "will return to the house. I'll speak to your father about your behavior."

Before he could stop her, Glorianna jerked her arm free from his grip and closed the distance between herself and the Dentons. "Mrs. Denton, I have done nothing wrong." Glory's tone showed her barely contained fury. "You have no right to speak to my father or to reprimand me."

Mrs. Denton leaned forward until her nose nearly touched Glorianna's. "You were out here in the middle of the night kissing my daughter's future husband. I realize your mother is dead, so I'm taking on a mother's responsibility by speaking to the captain about this. I want you to return to the house. Now."

Narrow eyes locked onto Conlon. "I will expect you at the house as soon as the drills are finished this morning. Chastity has a full day planned. You will be her escort." Mrs. Denton whirled about before either one could speak and sailed back toward the camp.

Chastity smirked at Glorianna and sidled closer to Conlon. "I'll see you soon. Bring Nina and Champ. We'll start with a long ride by ourselves." At her laugh of triumph, Conlon's hands balled into fists. He gritted his teeth, knowing he couldn't hit her, but picturing it anyway. Chastity sashayed after her mother.

"Glory, I'm sorry." He reached out to embrace her.

She stepped away. "Leave me alone." Tears ran down her cheeks. Her voice cracked. "I hate that woman. I hate Chastity, too. Somehow, I'll get even." She turned and ran away from the camp.

"Glory, wait," Conlon called after her. The sound of the bugle call from the camp told him he had no time to chase after Glorianna. After drills he would find her and settle this matter. Then he sighed, remembering. After drills he had to escort Chastity.

❧

Blinded by tears, Glorianna stumbled off into the desert. She had to get away. Away from Conlon. Away from the Dentons. Away from all the misery she felt inside. A paloverde tree, its green branches waving in the breeze, gave her a shaded sanctuary. She sank to the ground, burying her face in her hands. Deep, racking sobs shook her body.

What am I to do? she thought. *What will that woman do next? Can she make Conlon marry Chastity?* The memory of the kiss stilled her tears. Her first kiss. Her first wonderful kiss. She hadn't wanted the moment to end. Her heart pounded at the remembrance. She longed to be back with Conlon. She wanted to feel his arms around her again. She needed the comfort of his closeness.

Mother, I wish you were here. You would know how to handle this. Whom can I turn to now? Thoughts of Fayth, her friendship and kindness, made Glorianna sit up and wipe the traces of tears from her face. "Fayth," she spoke aloud. "She'll listen. I know she can help."

A short while later, she slipped quietly through the gates, avoiding the drills being performed on the parade ground. Dust hung heavy in the air from the horses milling around. The dust would help to hide her from the prying eyes of Mrs. Denton and Chastity. She circled around to the houses, hoping no one would notice her. She didn't want anyone to know where she was until she had talked to Fayth.

At the Holwells' she knocked, then pushed the door open. "Fayth?" she called.

"Glory, is that you?" Fayth's stepped from Alyce's room, a welcoming smile lighting her face. "Come on in. What are you doing here? I thought you'd be watching Conlon on the parade ground." Fayth pulled chairs together for them to sit in.

"Why aren't you out watching the drills?" Glorianna

avoided Fayth's question with one of her own.

"Alyce isn't feeling well. It's nothing serious. She's asleep now," Fayth hurried to add. She put a hand on her stomach. "Besides, this one is objecting to everything I eat. I wasn't sure I wanted to lose my breakfast in front of the whole camp."

Leaning forward, Fayth took Glorianna's hand in hers. "Is something wrong?" she asked, concern softening her voice.

Despite her resolve to be strong and not cry, Glorianna's throat began to tighten and tears welled in her eyes. She clasped her hands together, digging her nails into her palms, fighting her emotions. Then, Fayth's arms were around her and the dam broke. For long minutes she cried, unable to stop.

"I'm sorry," Glorianna hiccuped, wiping her eyes and nose with a handkerchief Fayth handed her. "I always seem to cry on your shoulder."

"I don't mind," Fayth laughed. "I think that's why God made shoulders. They're a wonderful place to support someone in need of comfort." She reached out to brush a strand of hair back from Glorianna's face. "Do you want to talk about it now?"

Glorianna took a deep breath and began in a shaky voice. She told about the strain of the last three weeks, trying to be nice to a tyrant, sharing a bed with Chastity, listening to Chastity's bragging about Conlon, and finally the heartache of not knowing how Conlon felt.

As she related the morning's events, anger replaced the hesitancy she'd been expressing. She told Fayth about Conlon's kiss, Mrs. Denton's accusations, and Chastity's parting words. "Can she really make him marry her daughter?"

"Glorianna, look at me," Fayth insisted. "Conlon is a strong man. Maybe a weaker man would give in to Mrs. Denton's demands, but he won't. He loves you, and I know his feelings for Chastity don't even begin to resemble love."

An inner rage welled up. Glorianna spat out, "I hate her. I

hate them both. Somehow, I'll get revenge on them."

Fayth sat back, a startled look on her face. "I don't think that's the answer. Perhaps we need to pray about this."

Glorianna stood and began to pace the room, fighting the urge to lash out at her friend. "I don't want to pray about it. I'm not sure God even cares about me anymore."

"Oh, but God does care about you." Fayth's eyes filled with tears.

Glorianna sank back into her chair and grasped Fayth's hands. "I didn't mean to hurt you. I'm just confused about God."

"You didn't hurt me." Fayth wrapped her hands around Glorianna's. "It's God you hurt."

"Well, God has hurt me plenty, too." She hated sounding like a petulant child, but she couldn't hold it in anymore. "He took my mother from me. We prayed every day for her to get well and she died. He wanted me to marry Kendrick and look what happened. Why should I even try to pray anymore?"

"Glorianna, do you know what the Bible says about heaven? It says there will be no more sickness. God answered your prayer to heal your mother. She's in a place where there is no pain or tears or sickness. Don't you agree?"

At Glorianna's reluctant nod, Fayth continued, "As for Kendrick, you told me you were wrong. Remember, after you were hurt in the storm? You admitted it had been you wanting him, not God wanting him for you."

"But, still," Glorianna's voice was almost a whisper. "He brought the Dentons here. I can't take this."

"God always allows trials. They're not a punishment, but meant to strengthen our faith." Fayth squeezed her hand. They sat quietly for a few minutes, and then Fayth spoke again. "I want to ask you something, Glorianna. I don't want to make you angry, but I have to know."

"What is it?"

"This may sound funny, but I feel I need to know if you're a Christian."

Glorianna straightened and tugged at her hands. "Of course, I'm a Christian! I've always been one."

Fayth held her fingers tight. "But, how do you know?"

"Well, I was born in a Christian home." Glorianna wanted to feel indignant, but for some reason she knew she needed to hear what Fayth wanted to say. "My parents have always attended church whenever possible. So have I. And I pray and read my Bible. I even help others. You know, doing good deeds."

Fayth shook her head, a look of concern crossing her face. "That isn't what makes a Christian. Who you know, or what you do, doesn't make you a follower of Jesus. Praying and reading the Bible are good, but that's not where salvation comes from."

"But, the church. . ."

"Church attendance doesn't make you a Christian, either."

Glorianna stared down at her hands clasped with Fayth's. She wanted to be angry, but for some reason she only felt confused. Was there something more to being a Christian that she'd missed all these years? A vague memory of her mother talking about salvation and choices surfaced. Had her mother tried to talk to her like this? Was God trying to get her attention?

"Do you know who General Crook is?" Fayth asked.

Surprised at the change in questions, Glorianna looked up at her friend. "I've heard of him. Conlon talked about meeting him."

"That's right." Fayth smiled. "You know who General Crook is, but do you know him personally?"

"Of course not," Glorianna said. "He's never been here or back east where we were. How could I know him?"

"The point I want to make," Fayth continued, "is that it's one thing to know who someone is and quite another to know him personally. It's the same with Jesus. You may know Who Jesus is, but to be a Christian you need to know Him personally. Do you?"

"I don't know." She took a deep breath. "You mean all these years I thought it was right to do good works and it wasn't?"

"Oh, no, it's always right to do good to others," Fayth assured her. "But, if we could get to Heaven by our good works, church attendance, or anything that we can do ourselves, then Jesus wouldn't have had to die on the cross for our sins. But Scripture tells us, 'For by grace are ye saved through faith; and that not of yourselves: it is the gift of God: Not of works, lest any man should boast.' "

"So, salvation is a gift?"

"That's right." Fayth smiled. "The Bible says that none of us deserves salvation. But God knew that from the beginning, and He provided a way for us."

"I want to know Him." Glorianna tightened her hold on Fayth's hands. A sudden urgency gripped her. "Tell me how, please."

"It's very simple. Do you believe Jesus died on the cross to take away your sins?"

Glorianna nodded, unable to speak.

"Do you believe God raised Him from the dead?"

"Yes, I believe that." The words barely made their way past the lump in her throat.

"Then all you have to do is ask Jesus into your heart."

As one, the two friends knelt by their chairs. They took turns praying, Glorianna's prayer hesitant yet joyful, Fayth's sure and thankful. Time seemed to stand still. Glorianna felt a healing and peace that she had never before known. Was this what her mother had talked about? This must be the peace that comes from knowing God.

Two hours later, Glorianna walked home. She felt as if her feet never touched the ground. The sky looked bluer and the desert more beautiful than she remembered. She looked forward to seeing how God would work things out. She had an assurance now that He would always care for her.

"Glorianna," her father's booming voice startled her from her reverie.

"Yes?" She smiled at him, ignoring the frown on his face.

"I've been looking for you. We need to talk. Please come to my office."

As they crossed the parade ground, Glorianna noticed Chastity and Conlon returning from their morning ride. Chastity patted her hair and grinned wickedly at Glorianna. Conlon flashed her a smile that set her heart racing. Suddenly, she couldn't wait to tell him about her new relationship with Jesus. She knew he had the same closeness and would be happy to hear about hers. For once, she wasn't jealous of Chastity for riding Nina or for being with Conlon. God was in charge, and He cared for her.

Mrs. Denton stood on the porch of her father's office. A smug look settled on her face at the sight of Glorianna and her father. She stepped forward to intercept them.

"Captain, would you like me to assist you with your daughter? I understand it's difficult for a father to reprimand his child. I'm more than willing to help."

Glorianna calmly watched her father face Mrs. Denton. She stood nearly as tall as he did, yet he didn't appear overwhelmed by her. "I believe I can handle this, Mrs. Denton. I thank you for your concern."

With that, he crossed over to his office and beckoned Glorianna to come in. For the first time since praying with Fayth, she began to doubt God's ability to work this out. Looking at her father's smoldering eyes, she couldn't help but tremble. *Dear God, please help me remember I'm Your child now. Help me to trust You, no matter what happens,* she prayed as her father shut the door with a resounding thud.

sixteen

Glorianna tried to still her trembling. She'd seen her father
this angry only once before. She thought of the time a few
years earlier, before her mother had gotten too sick to remain
out west at the various cavalry posts. Her father had been stationed at Camp Apache, up near where the Black River and
the White Mountain River join. The countryside, with its
stately pines, canyons, and tall mountains, took her breath
away. But the Apaches and wildlife in the area could be dangerous. Going outside the camp was strictly forbidden.

Glorianna, never one to follow the rules, wanted to explore
the forest. Innocently enough, she slipped away one afternoon, planning to climb to the top of the closest mountain.
Somehow, she managed to get turned around. Night fell and
she had no idea what direction to turn. After hours of searching, the soldiers from the camp found her and carried her
home.

Her mother wept while her father paced the floor, ranting
about the danger of her thoughtless actions. When he calmed
down she realized his eyes were nearly as red as her mother's.
He wasn't so much angry with her as he was scared that something terrible could have happened.

Suddenly, Glorianna understood her father's anger. It wasn't
directed at her, but at her situation. She swung around to look
at him. Love shone in eyes that only moments before had been
smoldering with anger. Could that anger have been directed at
Mrs. Denton and not her?

"If not for the grace of God and my respect for the major's
leadership abilities, I would lock that woman away," her
father growled. He pulled her close in a tight, safe hug. "I'm
so sorry she's here, Kitten. I know how hard it is to put up

with her and with that spoiled daughter of hers. Please try to persevere."

He pulled back and looked at her. His warm hazel eyes glowed with love. Glorianna reached up and patted his cheek. How she loved her father. He had always been the best he could be, even when it meant he had to be away from his family.

"Daddy, I'm sorry I said things to Mrs. Denton earlier that upset her. I have tried to be respectful." She sighed. "It isn't always easy."

He chuckled. "Yes, I'll certainly agree with that."

"I will apologize to her. I promise."

"You will?"

Her father's surprise reminded Glorianna of how self-serving and demanding she'd always been. "I know I've been difficult. I'm sorry." She took a deep breath and stepped back from her father. Looking him in the eye, she straightened to her full height. "I'm a different person now." She paused, trying to figure how to word what she needed to say. Then, with a short prayer for guidance, the words seemed to flow as she told him about her time with Fayth and the giving of herself to the Lord.

"Oh, Kitten." Her father hugged her again. This time she knew his tears were ones of joy. "I can't tell you how many times your mother and I prayed for this. I know she's in heaven rejoicing with the angels. Thank you for telling me."

He held her away and looked at her for a long time. "Now, what are we going to do about the Denton ladies?"

Glorianna tilted her head to the side and studied her father. "I think we should treat them like we would want to be treated, and let God do the rest. For my part, I'll try not to be jealous of Chastity. I'll be as nice as I can to Mrs. Denton." She paused and tapped a finger on her lip. "And, I believe I'll avoid them as much as possible so I can maintain a Christian attitude."

They both laughed, although they tried to keep it quiet so Mrs. Denton wouldn't hear them. She was sure to be standing outside waiting to see how their "talk" had gone.

Leaning close, her father spoke in a low tone. "I think we should sit down and discuss this. After all, she'll think you're getting a long lecture. That should make her happy."

For the next hour, they talked about camp life, the Lord, her mother, and myriad other things they never made the time to talk about. Glorianna warmed to her father's good advice and wonderful sense of humor, although they had to remember to laugh quietly.

"Try to look contrite," her father whispered as he prepared to open the door.

Glorianna forced her eyes to open wide, attempting a surprised look. "Me, look contrite?"

He grinned. "You were always a good actress. I'm sure you can do it."

She wrinkled her nose and crossed her eyes, watching him struggle to maintain his composure. He opened the door. Mrs. Denton shot up from the chair near the door. A frown drew her features into a hound dog expression. Glorianna wondered for a moment if she would begin to bark, then banished the thought before it became her undoing.

"I do hope the matter of Glorianna's improper behavior is settled, Captain." Mrs. Denton lifted her chin, speaking in an imperious tone.

Glorianna stepped forward, halting before the tyrannical woman. "I do want to apologize for any problems I've caused, Mrs. Denton. I appreciate your concern for me. I. . ." She felt a nudge from her father as she started to continue. He wouldn't want her to overdo it.

"Well, I do hope we won't have any more incidents like this morning. If you need an example to follow, you can watch my Chastity. She's a wonderful daughter." Mrs. Denton's face twisted into what she must have thought was a smile. "I know your mother was sick and probably unable to teach you as she should. That accounts for your lack of manners. I'll be happy to fill in."

Anger at the mention of her mother's lacking anything

swelled up inside. Her father, as if seeing the danger, spoke up. "I'm sure Glorianna will be fine now, Mrs. Denton. I promise to keep a closer eye on her. You seem to have your hands full watching your own daughter. I've noticed her forward behavior."

Mrs. Denton narrowed her eyes, staring at Captain Wilton. "Thank you for your concern, Captain," she said, before she turned and stalked away.

That afternoon, Glorianna curled up with her mother's Bible. Her mother used to spend hours reading and making notes. Now those observances spoke to her about her mother's desire to live her life in a way that pleased God. After rereading Ephesians 2:8 and 9 she had to stop reading and talk with God.

God, thank You for my salvation. I feel like I ought to do something to pay for this, but You say in the Bible it's a gift from You. Please be patient with me as I learn. I want to trust You with my life.

Your Word says here in verse 10 that You have good works for me to do. God, I want to do that, but You need to show me what those works are. Fayth says I need to start by seeing people the way You see them. If that's right, Lord, then it won't be easy. How can I possibly care for Chastity and her mother? Especially Chastity. She's trying her best to steal Conlon away from me. I love him, Lord. Please help me to see a good part or maybe some reason why I should love Chastity.

Tears ran down her cheeks. She tried to think of a redeeming quality for Chastity, but nothing came to mind. As she continued to read and pray, she marveled at the way the Bible made sense to her now, when it used to be so confusing. She felt like she'd never read these words before.

Late that afternoon, Glorianna hurried to Fayth's house to help get Alyce ready to go to the river. She'd lost track of time and knew the other ladies were already waiting by the stables.

"Fayth, are you ready?" she called through the open door.

A wailing cry was her only answer. She stepped in, calling again, heading to Alyce's room. Inside, Fayth, her hair in disarray, her face worn and tired, rocked her flushed child.

"Fayth, is she all right?"

A tired smile lit Fayth's face. "Her fever is higher now. I won't be going with you today."

"I'll stay and help you." Glorianna felt bad for not checking back in after this morning.

"No, you go," Fayth insisted. "I don't think Alyce will agree to let you hold her right now. Besides, Timothy will be here soon. He'll help out."

Panic stricken, Glorianna said, "But, I can't go to the river without you. What will I do about Chastity? I need you there."

"Glory, you don't need me. You have Jesus. Just listen to Him."

Glorianna prayed all the way to the ambulance, trying to find a reason to stay behind. *God, I know You want me to trust You and so I will. Please help me.* She looked up to see Chastity sitting astride Nina, so close to Champ that her knee occasionally brushed against Conlon's. The look of defiance on her face grated on Glorianna.

She swallowed her pride, forcing a smile. "I'm glad you like Nina, Chastity. It's nice you're willing to give her some exercise." A look of astonishment crossed Chastity's face. Glorianna climbed into the wagon with the other women.

The trip to the Verde River was miserable. Glorianna spent her time trying to ignore Mrs. Denton's loud lecturing to the wagon's occupants, and her daughter's obvious flirting. At least she could tell Conlon would rather be just about anywhere than riding with Chastity.

At the river, she moved away from the others, needing to be alone. The refreshing water not only cooled her physically, but soothed her ragged emotions as well. She dipped her head beneath the surface, rubbing her fingers through her tangled hair, washing the dirt free.

"I suppose you're trying to figure how you can get more time alone with Conlon." Chastity's snotty voice greeted her as she lifted her head out of the water. "My mother will be watching for you to sneak off and meet him in the mornings. That ploy won't work anymore."

"I didn't sneak off this morning." Glorianna tried to keep her tone even. "I simply went for a walk and met him."

"Are you saying you weren't in the habit of meeting him?"

"We enjoy watching the sunrise together. There's nothing wrong with that."

"I think there's something wrong with a young lady's spending so much time with a man when they aren't chaperoned."

"We weren't exactly alone." Glorianna struggled to control her temper. "After all, the night guards were watching. Besides, what about your rides together? You don't have a chaperone."

"Well. . .we. . .we aren't sitting together on a rock. Or kissing. . . ," Chastity sputtered.

Glorianna scooped some of the water in her hands and rubbed her face. Maybe the water would cool her anger. *God, I still can't find anything to love about her. Please, help me.*

Remember your childhood, came to her as clearly as if a voice had spoken out loud. She ducked under the water again to get a moment to think. What about her childhood? Then, understanding came in a rush. The years of constant moving, going to different forts and camps where there were only adults and few, if any, children. The terrible loneliness and longing for a friend. She remembered how glad she was to finally be back east where she and Kathleen could be friends.

She burst up from the water, catching Chastity unaware. The forlorn look on the girl's face confirmed her suspicions. *Thank You, God, for showing me the answer.*

"Tell me, Chastity," she said, watching the girl's expression closely. "Have you and your mother always followed your father wherever he was stationed?"

"Of course. What's wrong with that. Didn't you?"

"When I was young we did." Glorianna tried to pick her words with care. "Then, when my mother got sick, we had to go back east. We were there two years before she died."

"So?"

Glorianna took a deep breath. "The one thing I missed the most out here, the thing my father couldn't provide, was another girl my age. I didn't have a close friend until I took care of my mother. Then, my cousin Kathleen and I became best friends." She noted the look of longing that flitted across Chastity's face. "Have you ever had someone like that, Chastity?"

"My mother is my friend." Chastity looked over toward her mother and the other women.

"My mother was my friend, too," Glorianna said. "But didn't you ever want to be close to a girl your age? Someone to share a joke with or someone to stay up all night talking to?"

Chastity remained silent for a long time, still staring at the other women. Finally, she scooped water from the river, running her hands over her face. When she turned back to Glorianna her shiny eyes spoke of tears unshed. "I don't need a friend." Her voice was a hoarse whisper.

She began to edge away. The other women were moving to leave the river and Chastity started to follow them.

Before she could get too far, Glorianna called softly, "If you want a friend, I'm willing to be one."

Chastity stopped and turned toward her. "Why?" she asked bluntly.

"Why what?"

"Why would you want to be my friend?"

Glorianna tried to think from Chastity's point of view. Since arriving at Camp MacDowell, she had done nothing but torment Glorianna. She'd gone out of her way to steal Conlon, tried to alienate her father, and, in general, done her best to give Glorianna a bad name around the camp. She knew Chastity couldn't understand an offer of friendship under those circumstances.

Her heart pounding in nervous fear, Glorianna said, "I know I haven't been friendly to you before. This morning, my life changed. I gave my life to Jesus, and now I want to try to be like Him. I know I always needed a friend, and I'm sure Jesus wants me to be that to you."

Chastity whirled away and waded from the river. Glorianna followed, wondering if there was some other way that she could have answered the question better. At the top of the bank, Chastity waited for her. The others were already near the ambulance, laughing and chattering.

Speaking in a low tone, Chastity hissed, "I don't need your friendship. I don't want to hear about your religion, either. I have Conlon. He'll marry me soon and I won't need anyone else."

She stormed away toward the wagon. Glorianna didn't think she could hurt anymore if she'd been slapped across the face. *God, what did I do wrong? I tried to follow what You told me. It didn't work. How will I manage? I don't think I can stand to live if she marries Conlon.*

Trust Me, spoke a still, small voice.

seventeen

The rhythmic creak of the rocking chair sounded loud in the room's stillness. Glorianna laid her cheek against Alyce's hot forehead to see if her temperature had gone down. For the first time since she'd come by this evening, Alyce had ceased crying and fallen asleep. Although her face still bore the flush of fever, she felt a little cooler.

Removing the warm rag from Alyce's forehead, she dipped it in the basin of cool water on the stand beside her chair. She swirled the piece of toweling in the water before squeezing it out and placing it over Alyce's brow. The child barely moved. Only a slight puckering of her mouth showed she felt anything.

"Oh, Alyce," Glorianna whispered, "I hope love isn't so difficult for you." She couldn't quit thinking about Conlon. When they returned from the river, Chastity insisted that he come for her after supper so they could go for a walk. She knew he must have begged Timothy to go with them. Fayth wouldn't agree until Glorianna said she would stay with Alyce. After all, she'd pointed out, Fayth needed a break. A walk in the cool evening air would be refreshing.

The ache in her heart beat in a dull rhythm. She knew Conlon loved her, but would his love be strong enough to overcome Major and Mrs. Denton? Would they allow Chastity's wishes to dictate their lives and Conlon's? She wished her father could help, but his hands were tied when it came to superior officers. He could only make suggestions, and the Dentons didn't take kindly to suggestions about raising their daughter.

The sound of a door opening and muted voices drifted through the house. Fayth and Timothy stepped quietly into

Alyce's room. Fayth looked much better than she had earlier. Her cheeks, hollow and drawn from her inability to keep her food down, now had a bit of color.

"Is she sleeping?" Fayth's whisper barely reached across the room.

"She fell asleep about half an hour ago. I think her fever has gone down a little."

Fayth quietly crossed the room as Timothy slipped back into the front room. Glorianna could hear voices and wondered if Conlon had come back home with them.

"Let's put her in bed." Fayth pulled back the covers and centered the pillow. "It will probably be better if I don't take her. Do you think you can put her down?"

"I'll try." Glorianna stood, gritting her teeth against the ache in her arms. How did Fayth manage to hold this child for hours? She crossed to the bed, leaned over, and gently slipped Alyce into the bed. Alyce sighed and rolled to the side. The rag from her forehead dropped on the sheets. Fayth retrieved it and put it back in the bowl of water.

Touching Alyce's forehead, Fayth nodded. "I think you're right. She does feel cooler."

"You look much better, too. I think the walk was a good idea."

A high cackling laugh drifted through from the front room. Fayth's eyes met Glorianna's.

"We invited Conlon and Chastity to come in for awhile." Fayth glanced at the door and lowered her voice. "I think Timothy did it out of sympathy for Conlon. That girl needs some lessons in propriety."

"I don't think I can go out there." Glorianna sank down in the rocker. "I told you what happened at the river. How am I supposed to be civil to someone who only wants to make me look like a fool?"

Fayth pulled a chair over by Glorianna's. "Remember that while we were completely unlovable, God loved us. You have to follow His example. Jesus loved those who cursed

Him, spit on Him, and beat Him."

"You're right." Glorianna sighed. "If He can do that, surely I can love a lonely girl."

"I know you can." Fayth hugged Glorianna, then checked Alyce one more time. "Come on, Alyce is fine for now. Let's go visit."

Conlon and Timothy stood as they entered the room. Chastity edged her chair slightly closer to Conlon's. A smug smile twisted her features when she noticed Glorianna watching her. She settled back in the chair, her gaze never leaving Glorianna's. When Conlon sat down he would be within easy touching distance for Chastity.

"I see we need another chair." Conlon glanced around. "Here, Glory, why don't you take mine and I'll get another one. No, it's all right." He motioned Timothy to sit down. "I can get the chair."

Normally, Glorianna wouldn't have wanted to come so close to Chastity, but this time she knew it would keep Conlon from being next to the little vixen. Attempting her sweetest smile, she ignored the daggers flying from Chastity's eyes. "Why, thank you, Conlon." She crossed the room. Lowering herself to the chair, her elbow poked into Chastity's arm.

"Oh, excuse me." She lifted up and moved her chair. "I didn't realize your chair was so close."

"You did that on purpose," Chastity hissed.

Glorianna widened her eyes. "Did what?"

The anger faded from Chastity's face, replaced by a sugary smile that coated her features as Conlon walked toward them carrying a chair.

"You can sit next to me, Conlon." Chastity made it sound like an order.

"I think there's more room over here," Conlon replied, placing his chair on the other side of Glorianna. He settled into the chair, so close his sleeve brushed against her arm. She wanted to reach out and touch him, but knew it would only cause trouble between him and the Dentons.

Timothy asked about Alyce and a buzz of conversation drifted around Glorianna. She couldn't seem to concentrate on what they were saying. Her thoughts, instead, centered on the nearness of Conlon and her desire to tell him about her salvation. She forced herself not to fidget, picturing his excitement when she finally told him.

She didn't know how long her mind drifted, but a sudden uncomfortable silence in the room brought her back to the present. Sometime in the last few minutes, while her mind toyed with other thoughts, her fingers had become entangled with Conlon's. It felt so right that she hadn't even noticed and wasn't entirely sure he had, either. From the tension in the room and the look on her face, she knew Chastity was aware that they were holding hands.

Glorianna loosened her grip, thinking Conlon would allow her hand to drop. Instead he tightened his. Was he determined to make Chastity mad? Didn't he realize she had to sleep in the same room, the same bed, with the girl?

Chastity stood, red-faced, her eyes sparking with anger. "I believe I'll go on home. The hour is getting late." She stopped and looked back at Glorianna. "Come on, Mother will expect you home at the same time." Her eyes didn't leave their locked fingers.

"She's right." Glorianna stood. "I know Fayth is tired. Alyce may have another restless night, and they all need their rest."

"I'll walk the two of you home." Conlon, who stood when Chastity did, lifted his hand, pulling Glorianna a step closer. He didn't let her hand leave his. She wondered at his defiance of Chastity. *Oh, Lord, don't let him make trouble because of me,* she prayed.

The cool evening air wrapped around them as Conlon and Glorianna strolled the short distance to Glorianna's house. A pack of coyotes yipped and howled their nightly chorus, sounding as if they were next door rather than out in the desert. Chastity marched ahead of them, her back straight, head held high. She looked like a soldier on a mission.

Chastity stomped up to the door, flung it open, then turned to glare back at them. Without a word, she stepped inside, closing the door with a resounding thud. Conlon chuckled with what sounded like relief.

Glorianna squeezed his fingers. "You'd better be nice. Don't make me start laughing. If you do, I'll lie in bed giggling, and she'll know it's because of her."

"I'm not sure how you manage, Glory." Conlon's face was so close his breath tickled her ear. "Personally, I'm wishing I was anywhere but near Chastity Denton."

Glorianna turned to him, trying to ignore how close they were. "I have something to say." Now that the time had come she felt shy and nervous.

"I wanted to tell you what happened to me."

"I heard." His chuckle returned, louder this time.

"Did Fayth tell you?" Glorianna tried to hide her hurt.

Conlon looked puzzled. "Fayth didn't tell me. Timothy and some of the others told me yesterday. That was all the ladies could talk about—your dunking Chastity while pretending to fall. I forgot to mention it this morning."

She gasped. "You mean, they knew I did it on purpose?"

"Of course, they did. The men all got a good laugh. Too bad you didn't fall on Mrs. Denton, too."

"Conlon, stop." She glanced toward the house. "They'll hear you." She bit her lip trying not to succumb to laughter. "Besides, that's not what I have to tell you."

He took a deep breath as if trying to get himself under control. "I'm sorry. The picture of your holding Chastity under the water nearly did me in. What did you want to tell me?"

Suddenly, she couldn't put it into words. What would Conlon think? Would he think her foolish for thinking she was a Christian all these years only to find out she wasn't? Did it matter so much if she told him? *Confess with your mouth,* she could hear Fayth say.

"I prayed with Fayth today," she blurted out.

He tilted his head to one side, the shadows hiding his eyes from her. "Did you pray for Alyce?"

"No. . . I. . . Yes." She stopped, knowing she wasn't making any sense. She stepped back from him, pulling her hand free, hoping the distance would help to calm her thoughts.

"Fayth pointed out to me that, although I've always gone to church, I've never had a personal relationship with Jesus. We prayed about that." Twisting her fingers together, she waited for his laughter.

Strong arms engulfed her. Conlon crushed her against him in a fierce hug. "Oh, Glory, this is an answer to prayer. Thank you for telling me."

His genuine feelings touched her. Tears welled up in her eyes. "I thought maybe you would laugh."

He held her away. The rising moon glinted off the tears on his cheeks. "I can't tell you how happy I am about this. I can't tell you, but I can show you."

He dropped to one knee. Grasping her hands in his, he kissed her fingertips. "Glorianna, will you marry me? I'll talk to your father tomorrow morning. Tonight, I want to make sure you will have me."

She could barely talk. "Yes. Yes, I'll marry you, Conlon Sullivan."

He stood and pulled her into his arms. His kiss was sweet. She felt so safe and content held in his embrace.

"Glorianna Wilton, you get in here right now." Mrs. Denton's voice grated in the night.

"Why does she always interrupt?" Conlon squeezed her hand, then traced a finger down her cheek. "I'll see you in the morning. I'll talk to your father as soon as I can."

"Good night." Glorianna wanted to say more, but didn't dare with Mrs. Denton standing guard. Already she felt empty at his leaving. Dreamily, she brushed by Mrs. Denton and floated to her room. *Mrs. Conlon Sullivan, Glorianna Sullivan,* she thought. *It sounds perfect. Thank You, God.*

"It's about time you came inside." Chastity's petulant

whine brought reality crashing in. "What were you doing out there for so long? Kissing again?"

Glorianna felt like the smile she couldn't wipe from her face must certainly give her away. There was nothing Chastity could say that would take away this happiness. Conlon wanted to marry her.

"I suppose you think he's going to marry you." Chastity's words made Glorianna wonder if she'd read her mind. "Well, I'll tell you this, my father arrived early. He's here right now. By morning he'll have told Lieutenant Sullivan exactly what his orders are. Those orders don't include you."

For the first time since coming inside, Glorianna really looked at Chastity. Her eyes flashed anger, and possibly hatred. Her blond hair straggled around her face, which was covered with red blotches. Her lips were pinched into thin lines. She felt sorry for this girl, who had missed out on so much by focusing on herself.

Lord, help me talk to her. I don't know what to say. She doesn't want me for a friend, and I can't force my friendship on her. Help me to be like You, no matter what she says or does to me.

"I'm glad your father finally got here, Chastity. I know you wanted to see him. Maybe in the morning we can get some of this straightened out."

"There's nothing to straighten out," Chastity sputtered. "You think you have the right to waltz in here and claim the man who's going to be my husband. Well, you don't. The last time we were at Camp MacDowell it was decided that Conlon and I would marry."

"Did he propose to you?"

"No, he didn't propose. We had an understanding, though." Chastity glared at Glorianna. "He would have asked me to marry him by now, if you hadn't interfered."

"I don't know how I've done that." Glorianna turned away to pull on a nightdress, hoping to keep her anger down. *Lord, help me keep my tongue under control.*

"You don't consider meeting my intended in the middle of the night, holding hands with him, and kissing him as interfering?"

Glorianna blew out the lamp and climbed into bed beside Chastity. She bit her lip, determined to hold her angry thoughts and words at bay.

"You'll see," Chastity hissed in the silence. "Tomorrow my father will tell him what's what."

"Your father hasn't any authority over Conlon's personal life. Conlon is free to make his own decisions. That includes choosing for himself the woman he wants to marry."

"I suppose you think that will be you."

Glorianna ground her teeth together, fighting a losing battle for control. "I know it will be me." She couldn't keep the words inside. "He's never had feelings for you." As the words left her mouth, she longed to pull them back, but it was too late.

A sniffle sounded in the silence. Then Chastity spoke in a tear-filled voice. "Just wait until tomorrow. You'll see."

"Chastity, I'm sorry. I. . ."

"Leave me alone, Glorianna. I don't want to talk anymore."

Glorianna could feel the bed move as Chastity turned over. *Oh, Lord, I want to be like You, but I can't. I let my mouth get the best of me. Please, forgive me. Now I'll never be able to get Chastity to open up to me. I'm so sorry, and I'm so scared that she's right. Can her father really make Conlon marry her? Please, don't let that happen. Please.*

Sleep took a long time coming.

eighteen

Whistling slightly off key, Conlon strode toward the captain's office. He couldn't help whistling. Even though Glorianna hadn't gotten away to meet him this morning, he felt as if he were walking on air. She loved him. She wanted to marry him. Now the captain had summoned him to the office. This would be the perfect time to ask for his daughter's hand in marriage. Of course, he didn't doubt the captain's answer. After all, he had readily agreed to let him court her.

Leaping up the steps, he paused, amazed at the difference in the world around him. The sky stretched overhead like a taut blue canvas, blank, waiting for God to paint His signature for the day. Birds trilled, men shouted, horses called for their breakfast, all with a clarity of sound that hadn't been there before. The whole world gleamed with the knowledge of his and Glory's love for one another.

Nodding to the private who worked for the captain, Conlon knocked on the office door.

"Come in."

He pushed open the door and confronted the first bit of concern since rising this morning. Captain Wilton wasn't alone. Major Denton filled the office with his commanding presence. When had he arrived? Suddenly, Conlon felt a pinprick of dread worm its way inside his heart. Why had the captain summoned him?

"Good morning, Lieutenant. I'm sure you remember Major Denton."

Standing stiff, Conlon nodded at the major. "Yes, Sir. Good morning, Major. I'm glad to see you've arrived. I trust you and General Crook were able to round up the renegades?"

"General Crook is a remarkable man." Major Denton's voice rattled the walls. "We made short work of rounding up the Apaches and getting them back where they belonged."

"Lieutenant, please have a seat. There's a matter we need to discuss." Captain Wilton's voice sounded lackluster.

Conlon studied the captain as he lowered himself into the chair. Something was wrong. He could feel it. The captain's eyes were dull, his face drawn, and sadness hung over him like a pall. Conlon decided to sit quietly, waiting for the captain to tell him the bad news.

Major Denton's thunderous voice startled him. "I believe I've upset your captain this morning, Lieutenant. I've brought some news he hadn't expected. He doesn't seem to agree with me, but sometimes that's the way it is with the military."

Conlon swung around to face the major. The feeling of dread spread through his body like a disease, consuming him. He felt weighed down, as if his whole body were covered with lead.

"Those papers on the captain's desk are your transfer orders."

Once, in a fight at school, a boy had punched Conlon in the stomach, knocking the breath out of him. He had fallen to the ground, unable to breathe or respond at all. That same helpless, wheezing feeling overtook him now. The major's words dimmed and for a moment he feared he would not get hold of himself.

"Excuse me, Major." Conlon didn't care if he was interrupting. "What did you say?"

Major Denton laughed, tilting his head back and allowing a full throaty chuckle to issue forth. "I told you he'd be glad to get away from this post, Captain. This is the most forsaken country I've ever seen. Any soldier would be grateful to get a reprieve."

Conlon glanced at Captain Wilton. "Did I hear him right? Am I getting a transfer?" At the captain's nod, Conlon asked. "When? Where?"

"Your orders state immediately." The captain's voice echoed in the silence.

"Yes, Sir, Lieutenant." Major Denton slapped him on the back. "You'll enjoy Fort Lowell outside of Tucson. It's a great place. Most of all you'll enjoy being where my daughter is."

"Your daughter isn't there, Sir, she's here."

Major Denton laughed again. "Only for a short time. Right now, she and my wife are packing. They are leaving with us just as soon as we all get ready to head out."

Confusion and anger fought a battle inside him. Conlon stared at the major. "You mean I have to go now?"

"That's right. Your orders are immediate. I brought them in myself last night. Sorry there isn't more notice, but in the cavalry you have to be ready."

"But, I don't want to go to Fort Lowell," Conlon blurted, feeling stupid for coming up with such a weak statement. "I mean, I needed to talk to the captain about something personal this morning. I have some private matters to settle before I can leave here." He forced himself to stop babbling, fighting down the panic welling up inside.

"Son, I understand your private matters have to do with my daughter. We can discuss them on the way to Fort Lowell. We'll have plenty of time."

"Sir, the private matters have to do with the captain's daughter."

Major Denton chuckled. "I've heard she'll be mighty disappointed to see you and Chastity together, but she'll have to get used to the idea."

"But, Sir. . ." Conlon's objections died as the major dismissed him with a wave of his hand.

"Not now, soldier. We need to talk about your plans for leaving here."

Conlon bit his lip to keep from snapping at the major. Couldn't this oaf see that he wasn't interested in marrying his whiny daughter? He wanted to grab him by the shirtfront and set him straight. He looked at the captain, hoping he would intercede, yet he knew Captain Wilton could do nothing to countermand an order by a superior officer.

"But, don't we need to wait for a replacement for me?" Conlon asked, grasping for any excuse.

"No need for that," Major Denton said. "I brought a young lieutenant with me last night. He'll mature nicely under Captain Wilton's command."

"May I have a moment to speak privately with Lieutenant Sullivan, Major?"

"Certainly." Major Denton rose. "Don't take too long, though. My wife is anxious to leave. I'm sure they'll be ready within the hour, and the lieutenant still has to get his things packed."

Silence stretched tautly when the major closed the door behind him. Conlon forced himself to look up and meet the captain's sad eyes. How differently this moment was turning out compared to what he dreamed about last night.

"You wanted to talk to me?"

Conlon leaned forward in his chair, his elbows on his knees. "Last night I asked Glorianna to marry me. I told her I would speak to you this morning. I'd like your permission, Sir."

"You realize the Dentons expect you to marry Chastity."

"Yes, Sir." Conlon sat up straight, anger making him determined. "I've never once given Chastity or her parents any reason to suspect I would marry her. I've only done my duty by following orders and escorting her around. They have assumed things. I love your daughter. I want to marry her."

"How does Glorianna feel about this?"

"She loves me, too, Sir. Last night she agreed to become my wife. I can't leave now." Conlon noticed his fingers twisting his cap as if they had a mind of their own. He forced himself to stop. "Couldn't you at least get a delay in my orders, Sir?"

Captain Wilton sighed. "I don't know what I can do. I'll pray about it. Right now, you need to go pack. Let me see if there's any other way. You realize the Dentons are used to getting their way, don't you?"

Conlon stood, pulling his cap back on his head. "Yes, Sir, but there's also God's way. I believe He has a way to make this right. We'll both pray about it."

"Conlon?"

He stopped with his hand poised over the doorknob. The captain had never called him by his first name before. "Yes, Sir?"

"You have my blessing. I would be happy to have you for a son-in-law."

"Thank you, Sir."

In a daze, Conlon left the captain's office and crossed to his quarters. The sky had lost its brilliance, the birds' songs grated on his nerves, and he wanted to yell at God for not watching over him like He promised in Scripture. He'd waited all this time. He'd been patient, yet look what happened. For all the faithfulness he'd shown to God, God was turning His back. *Why,* he cried silently, *why did You let this happen? Just when Glorianna is willing to marry me, I'm jerked away like some puppet. How can any good come out of this?*

"Conlon?" Josiah's deep voice cut through his thoughts.

"Come in," Conlon called, not sure whether to be resentful of the intrusion or glad to have a friend when he felt so low.

"I heard." Josiah, always blunt, sank down on the cot.

Conlon continued to gather his things in silence, not knowing what to say. The hurt ate at him, stealing his reason, stealing his voice.

"You know God has a plan here." Josiah's statement hit a nerve.

"I know that's what the Bible says." Conlon couldn't hold back his anger. "I also know He told me to wait patiently. I did. Now look what I've got to show for it."

"And what would have happened if you'd not been so patient with Glorianna?" At Conlon's silence, Josiah continued. "You know very well you would have lost her. If it's meant to be, God will see things through. Trust Him and be patient, just like He asks."

"But, last night Glorianna said she would marry me. This morning I felt like God was in charge of everything. Then, I got my orders and all that changed."

"So, what's different?" Josiah asked quietly.

Conlon knelt on the floor in front of his bedroll. He covered his face with his hands. Josiah didn't interrupt his thoughts.

"You're right, Josiah," he sighed. "It isn't God Who changed. It's my outlook." He bowed his head and whispered, "Oh, God, I'm sorry I didn't trust You totally. Please see me through this. Help me to wait on You."

When he finished the prayer, he felt Josiah's arm around his shoulders. His friend knelt with him on the hard floor, praying for the guidance only God can give.

"Thank you," Conlon said, gruffly. "I don't know what I'll do without you, either."

Josiah grinned. "You won't have to be without me for long. My hitch is up in a couple of months. I'm planning to get out."

"You didn't tell me." Conlon couldn't suppress the surprise. "When did you decide this?"

"I've been praying about it for awhile," Josiah said. "I feel the Lord directing me to set up my own blacksmith shop in Tucson. I'll look you up when I get there."

"I'll look forward to it," Conlon spoke sincerely. "I just hope you'll be able to look up Glorianna and me."

"We'll keep praying about it. God brought you this far. Be patient and let Him do the rest."

❧

With tears in her eyes and a pain in her heart so severe she thought she might die, Glorianna watched the ambulance being packed. This morning, as soon as she got out of bed, Chastity blurted out the news that they were leaving, and Conlon had orders to go with them. The triumph in her eyes made Glorianna want to scratch the orbs from her face.

Chastity told her that she and Conlon would be married before Thanksgiving for sure. After all, there wasn't a parson anywhere around here, but in Tucson it wouldn't be hard to find one. Glorianna's stomach had been tied in knots ever since.

God, how could You allow this? I know Fayth says You allow trials, but haven't we gone through enough? I don't know how I can live life knowing Conlon is married to Chastity and not me. Please, God, I have the feeling if he leaves with them, I'll never see him again. Help me. Help us.

She clutched the handle of her parasol, not caring that it wasn't even tilted right to keep the sun off her face. What were a few freckles compared to life without Conlon? She wanted to rush to his quarters and beg him to stay. But that was foolish. He couldn't disobey orders. The matter was out of his hands. Even her father couldn't change things. She knew he had tried. She'd overheard him talking to the major.

Trust. The voice wove a soft pattern across her heart. *Lean not on thine own understanding.*

Lord, I know in my head I can trust You. But my heart won't listen. I feel like everything is falling apart. I feel like You're not in control.

Glorianna thought about Fayth and the Scriptures they'd discussed since she arrived at Camp MacDowell. Over and over, Fayth reminded her that you can't trust in your feelings, but you can trust in God's Word.

Okay, God, even though it seems hopeless, I want to trust You. Help me just to look at You and not at the circumstances around me.

"Well, I hear you won't be lonely." Chastity sauntered over from the wagon. "My father says he brought a new lieutenant with him. Maybe you can get him to marry you."

Glorianna wanted to wipe the smirk off Chastity's face. She closed her eyes and said a quick prayer. Peace flooded over her, filling every part of her with a sense of well-being, of knowing God could and would take care of everything.

"Chastity, I know you're lonely and need a friend," she said softly. "But I want you to stop and think about what you're doing. Forcing a man to marry you when he doesn't want to isn't the answer. Soon he'll turn bitter, and your life will be miserable."

Chastity's eyes narrowed and Glorianna hurried on before she interrupted. "I know somewhere the right man is waiting. Conlon isn't that man. Please don't make him do something that both of you will regret."

"You just want him for yourself," Chastity snapped. "I know he'll be happy once we're away from you. Mother and I plan to have the wedding as soon as we get to Tucson."

Chastity whirled and stalked back to the ambulance, where her mother directed the two soldiers loading their trunks. *God, I don't see how You can work this out,* Glorianna prayed, watching the duo prepare to leave. *I'm trying not to listen to my understanding, but to trust You.* She turned and trudged toward the stables, hoping to find Conlon before he left.

"Conlon?" He had his back to her, saddling Champ. She ached to touch him, to tell him it would be all right. She knew by the sag in his shoulders how discouraged he was.

"Glorianna." He swung around, not losing his grip on the cinch he was tightening.

"I heard you're leaving." She tried to say more, but the lump growing in her throat held back the words.

He nodded. "I tried to get out of it, but I can't." He dropped the cinch strap and reached for her. His arms wrapped tightly around her, pulling her close. "I'll miss you so much, my Morning Glory. Somehow, this will work out."

She gazed into his deep blue eyes that overflowed with love. "I love you," she whispered, then stepped back, hearing the major call for him. Watching him ride down the stable aisle, she felt like she were being torn in two. Was he right? Would this work out or was this the last time she would see him?

nineteen

The outline of the business district at Florence barely broke the skyline when Major Denton called a halt. Conlon watched the weary soldiers swing down from their equally tired mounts. They should have arrived at Florence yesterday, for the major and the ladies to take the stage to Tucson, leaving the cavalrymen to follow with their belongings at a more leisurely pace. None of them counted on the various mishaps that had beset them on the way.

On the morning of the second day, one of the wagon wheels dropped into a rut, splintering several spokes. It took hours to fix the wheel, and they traveled late to make up lost time. Then, this morning, they rose before dawn to resume the trip. In the predawn darkness, one of the horses pulling the ambulance stepped in a hole, breaking its leg. They lost even more time disposing of the horse and bringing in a replacement. What should have been a two-day trip had taken them three long days.

"Lieutenant."

Mrs. Denton's voice twisted the knot in his stomach. She had done nothing but complain over the delays. Between her bossiness and Chastity's whining about being uncomfortable, he wanted to throttle them both. How did the major stand it? Perhaps this explained why he spent so much time in the field.

"Yes, Ma'am?" Conlon tried to keep his voice polite as he kneed Champ closer to the wagon.

"Why are we stopping?" Mrs. Denton demanded. "We need to get on to Florence so Chastity and I can rest."

"I would assume we stopped to let the horses get their wind," Conlon tried to explain, knowing Mrs. Denton wouldn't be listening anyway. "We've been traveling hard, and the strain is telling on the horses. We'll be in Florence in time for you to catch the evening stage."

"Conlon, I need to get out and walk," Chastity whined. "I want someone to escort me." She tilted her head to one side, as if trying to look coy.

Reining Champ away from the wagon, Conlon called back, "I'll send someone to walk with you. Now, if you'll excuse me, I need to see the major." He quickly urged Champ to a faster pace, hoping they wouldn't call him back. Gritting his teeth, Conlon determined he wouldn't spend any more time with Chastity Denton than absolutely necessary. Nor would he cater to her whims. He didn't have to, now that his actions weren't hurting the captain.

"Lieutenant." Major Denton beckoned to him. "I've just heard that there's a detachment of soldiers from Fort Lowell in Florence. I want to ride ahead and see why they're there. Will you accompany me? I believe the ambulance will be well escorted without us."

Falling in beside the major, Conlon tried to remember what he had planned to say. All the arguments that came so easily last night disappeared now. *God, I need You to give me the words,* he prayed. *Please, don't let me offend this man. Prepare his heart to really hear what I have to say and to accept it. Thank You, Father.*

"You know, Sullivan, my wife and daughter seem determined to have a wedding the minute we arrive in Tucson." Major Denton glanced over at Conlon.

Conlon nodded, waiting to see what the major was leading up to. Had God already worked in this man's heart or was he going to help plan the wedding?

"When I mentioned your marrying my daughter, I thought I detected some reluctance on your part. Is that correct?"

Taking a deep breath, Conlon prayed again for the appropriate words. "Yes, Sir, you're right."

"I'm thinking you might have some feelings for the captain's daughter."

Conlon nodded again, not sure where this was leading.

"Why didn't you just say so? Why did you continue to escort my daughter?"

"Well, Sir, to be honest, I was concerned about the captain." At Major Denton's questioning look, Conlon continued. "The last time you were at Camp MacDowell, I tried to discourage Chastity. If you remember, Sir, Captain Wilton came under fire for my behavior."

"I do recall some of that," Major Denton admitted. "My apologies. I realize my wife and daughter can be rather determined once they set their minds to something. However, I've been doing a lot of thinking in the past few days." He paused, his dark eyes watching Conlon. "I don't want my daughter marrying a man who doesn't want her. That would make for a disastrous marriage. Don't you agree?"

"Yes, Sir."

"I've decided to intervene. I know my wife. She won't like it, and Chastity will cry for awhile, but I think it's best if you don't marry her."

"Thank you, Sir." *Thank You, God,* Conlon added silently. "I'm sure your daughter will find the right man some day, but I'm not him. I can't marry her when my heart belongs to another. I hope you can see that, Sir."

Major Denton pulled his horse to a halt. He stretched out his hand and Conlon grasped it in a firm handshake. "I understand completely, Lieutenant."

"Thank you," Conlon repeated. "I am afraid, Sir, that it won't be easy to convince Mrs. Denton and Chastity to call off the wedding."

"You let me handle that." Major Denton chuckled. "I'll break the news and then ride out for a week or two with some soldiers. I've found it's the best way to handle those two."

At the outskirts of Florence, Major Denton gestured to a group of cavalrymen gathered by their horses. Conlon followed him as he urged his horse to a canter, changing direction to intercept the troops. They looked as if they were preparing to mount up and ride out until Conlon and the major came riding over.

A young lieutenant handed over the reins of his horse to another cavalryman and walked over to meet them. He saluted as the major dismounted.

"Lieutenant Rourke, Sir."

"Lieutenant." Major Denton returned his salute and finished the introductions. "What are you men doing so far from Fort Lowell? Is there trouble?"

"We were tracking a soldier, Sir. We had one who'd gone bad. He was coming up for trial and he broke out. He killed the soldier guarding him and escaped."

"Did you catch him?" Major Denton asked.

"No, Sir, we tracked him all the way to the Superstition Mountains. We lost him in the canyons there."

"That's a miserable place to try to find someone," Major Denton said.

"True," said Lieutenant Rourke. "We finally gave up after we lost one of our men."

"How's that? It wasn't Indians, was it?" Major Denton looked tense.

"No, Sir." Lieutenant Rourke paled slightly, as if the memory of what happened still plagued him. "One of the men left camp by himself. A cougar got him." The lieutenant rubbed a hand over his face. "We'd heard the cat scream the night before, but didn't think about it being out in the daylight. We couldn't understand why it was taking O'Reilly so long to get back. When we found him it was too late."

"We were tracking some Indians in the Superstitions a few weeks back and heard a cougar." Conlon shuddered at the thought of losing one of his men that way.

Lieutenant Rourke choked for a moment before he could continue. "O'Reilly was a good man. One of the best. Judging by the tracks, the cat was a big one. We decided to leave Smith to the cougar. I didn't want to risk any more men."

"Who?" Conlon tried to calm his sense of panic. "Who were you chasing?"

Major Denton and the lieutenant were both staring at him. "The man's name is Smith, Dirk Smith. I believe he used to be at Camp MacDowell so maybe you know him."

Conlon felt the world shift beneath his feet. Dirk! He was back in the area and Glorianna didn't know. What if he tried to get to her? He turned to the major, urgency taking the place of everything else.

"Major Denton, I have to go back to Camp MacDowell. We originally sent Dirk Smith to Fort Lowell because he attacked the captain's daughter twice. The first time he was drunk, but the second time he fully intended to take advantage of her. He may try again."

Major Denton studied him for a long minute. "Go on back, Sullivan. I'll take care of your orders. I'll have them delayed for a few weeks. We'll send you notice."

"Be careful of him, Lieutenant," Rourke warned. "He's a dangerous man. He's killed once and probably won't hesitate to do it again."

Running to mount Champ, Conlon prayed, *Please, God, protect Glorianna. Don't let that madman get his hands on her.* Anger began to build as he thought of Dirk's touching Glorianna. He had to get back in time.

❧

"Glorianna?" Fayth called through the open door. "May we come in?"

"Go'wy." Alyce's high voice mimicked her mother.

Glorianna smiled as she crossed the front room to the door. "Of course, you may come in." It felt good to smile. She hadn't done much of that since Conlon rode off with the Dentons, taking her heart with him. Life now consisted of a constant ache within as she longed for his return.

"How are you doing?" Fayth's steady gaze seemed to look right through her façade and uncover the misery beneath.

"I miss him so much." Glorianna fought back the tears. "I'm

so glad I have God now. Despite all the hurt, deep down I have a peace I can't explain. I know things will work out, I just don't know if they will work out the way I want them to."

"At least you know things will work out God's way. Right?" Fayth asked softly.

"Yes," Glorianna said. "But, of course, I do wish I had one more chance to dunk Chastity in the river. Maybe I wouldn't let her up so soon," she teased.

Fayth laughed. "Sometimes I think I'd like to help you with that. Oh, by the way, I came to bring you a letter. Timothy brought it by a little while ago."

Glorianna held the cream-colored envelope in her hand for a moment, savoring its heaviness. "It's from Kathleen. I miss her so much. She was my only friend until you." She tore open the letter before her eyes got too watery. She had been crying entirely too much lately.

"If you want, we'll leave so you can have time with your letter."

"No, please stay," Glorianna urged Fayth. She pulled Alyce up on her lap. "Besides, I won't let Alyce go, so you have to stay. Let me tell you what Kathleen has to say."

She opened the letter and read for a minute. A blush heated her cheeks. "Oh, my." She slapped a hand over her mouth. "It seems that Kendrick and Melissa are married now."

"So soon?" Fayth asked. "I thought they weren't getting married for a couple of months.

"That's what everyone else thought, too. But, it seems Melissa's father visited Kendrick with a shotgun and the two of them were married very quickly."

Fayth gasped and covered her mouth with her hand. "I hate to say this, but I'm glad you didn't marry him if he's that kind of man."

Glorianna hugged Alyce against her. "I thought I'd be upset when they got married, but I find I don't care at all. I believe that if I had gotten to know Kendrick I may not have

liked him so much. I realize now I only liked him because all the other girls did. That's a poor reason to marry someone."

"Unfortunately, when we're young we can be easily influenced that way. I wonder if God brought you out here to get you away from that situation."

"I know now that God has my best interests at heart. I only want to trust Him, even though it's hard for me not to tell Him what I think those best interests are."

Fayth grinned. "I think we all have that problem."

Slipping the unfinished letter in her pocket, Glorianna tickled Alyce, making her giggle. Alyce's deep chuckle was contagious and they all laughed.

"I've been moping around here long enough," Glorianna declared. "Why don't we go for a ride. I haven't ridden Nina since Chastity took her over. Would you go with me?"

After leaving Alyce with Mrs. Peterson, Fayth and Glorianna hurried to the stable for their horses. They planned a late evening meal, which would give them a couple of hours to ride.

"Are you sure you'll be able to ride?" Glorianna asked again. "I don't want you to do this if it will hurt the baby."

"Don't worry about this baby. He's too feisty to be hurt by anything as simple as a horseback ride. I think getting away for awhile will be the best thing for me."

Glorianna settled into Nina's easy walk, relaxing completely for the first time in days. She hadn't been this direction before. This road led to Pinal City and the Florence turn-off. Conlon had ridden this road only four days ago. Was he in Tucson by now? Had Chastity made him marry her? She pushed the thoughts from her head before worry set in once more. Trust. That's what God wanted her to do.

"This is a beautiful time of day." Glorianna savored the peacefulness of the desert. "I love to watch the rabbits and coyotes. I don't even mind a snake if it keeps its distance."

"Oh, look." Fayth pointed ahead and to the left. A herd of antelope raced over a slight rise. They bounded effortlessly

across the desert, leaping over bushes and weaving around the cactus. Pulling the horses to a halt, they watched the graceful animals until they were out of sight.

"I wonder what startled them." Fayth frowned. "Maybe we should head back to the camp."

"But we still have at least an hour to ride." Glorianna didn't want to give up this time. "Why do you want to go back? Are you feeling ill?"

"No." Fayth glanced over her shoulder. "I just feel uneasy for some reason." She shrugged. "I'm being silly, I guess."

They rode down the side of the hill where the antelope had run. At the bottom stood a clump of trees. As they approached the trees, Nina pricked her ears forward. She nickered softly.

"What is it, girl?" Glorianna patted Nina's neck. "What's out there that interests you?"

"It might be me." Dirk stepped from behind a tree, grabbing Nina's bridle so swiftly Glorianna couldn't react.

twenty

Heart pounding, Glorianna jerked futilely on the reins. Her worst nightmare stood before her. A gash, crusted over with dirt and dried blood, covered part of one unshaven cheek. Judging from the redness surrounding the wound, infection had set in. Brown patches of what might be dried blood spotted his clothing. She shuddered, not wanting to know if it was Dirk's or someone else's. Bile rose in her throat and she covered her nose to ward off the stench of his unwashed body. His dark-circled, haunted eyes glared at her. Her stomach churned. Where had he come from?

"Let go of my horse." Glorianna hoped to keep her voice steady. Then, before he could say anything, she called, "Go, Fayth, get help."

Dirk's hand snaked out even as she uttered the words. He grabbed Fayth's horse before she could turn him. "Not so fast," he warned. "You're both coming with me." Blackened teeth showed through his grin.

"My husband and the others from the camp expect us back soon, Mr. Smith." Fayth's words steadied Glorianna. "You won't get away with this."

A mirthless laugh filled the air around them. "I heard the little lady say you still had an hour before you had to be back. That will give us plenty of time to put some distance between us and the camp."

Dirk jerked the reins away from them and led the horses into the trees. A horse, tethered to a tree, waited for him. Dirk mounted, never letting go of their reins. He turned his horse east, riding parallel to the road, but off of it.

"Where are you taking us?" Glorianna bit her lip, knowing he heard the fear in her voice.

Dirk grinned back at her. "I have a little place all picked out for you and me. We'll be together from now on, so you'd best get used to the idea."

"But, what about Fayth? You don't need to drag her along."

He chuckled malevolently. "Oh, I'll let her go soon enough. Then, it'll just be the two of us. I didn't know you were so eager."

Glorianna shuddered. She looked at Fayth, hoping desperately for a way out of this. Fayth's closed eyes and moving lips reminded her that she had other help with her at all times. How could she have forgotten?

God, help us, her prayer screamed out inside her head. *You can't let this happen.* Taking a calming breath, she tried to gather her thoughts.

Jesus, I know You are my Protector, my Shield, and my Help in time of trouble. You asked me to trust You and lean not on my own understanding. But where are You? How can You allow something like this? What about Fayth and the baby?

Glorianna bit her lip. She knew she was repeating herself. She closed her eyes and reassurance gradually eased her fear. She knew Fayth would be praying, too. *Oh, Lord, if only Conlon were here. Why did he have to leave? But, there I go, questioning You again. Please forgive all my doubts.* A gentle peace crept over her. She sighed, feeling as if someone was there with her, holding her close. *Thank You,* she said, silently.

"Are you all right?" Glorianna asked Fayth.

"Shut up," Dirk barked. "If you talk, I'll have to gag you."

Glorianna bit her lip, wondering if she had turned pale. The thought of being gagged with some of Dirk's clothing almost made her retch.

When he turned back around, Fayth reached over and quickly squeezed her hand. "I'm fine," she mouthed the words silently. Her smile helped Glorianna relax. *God is in charge,* she told herself. *Remember that.*

Dirk set a fast pace, heading toward the Superstition

Mountains. The road to Florence was a ribbon of brown in the distance. They could only see pieces of it when they topped a rise in the desert. Each time, Glorianna looked at the road with longing. A quiet despair began to settle over her as she wondered if anyone would ever find them. She remembered Conlon's saying how hard it was to find Indians once they made it to the Superstitions. There were myriad places to hide there.

Two hours later, the sun dipping low in the west, Glorianna knew she had to speak up. Fayth could barely stay upright in the saddle. Pain etched pale lines in her face. "Mr. Smith, we have to stop. Fayth can't go on like this."

Reining in his horse, Dirk turned to look at them, his eyes filled with anger. "We have to get to the mountains. We aren't stopping just because one of you can't keep up." He swiveled back around and jerked the horses' reins to start again.

Fayth's eyes filled with tears. Her whitened fingers gripped the saddle as if trying to ease the jolting gait. Each time her horse stumbled on the uneven ground, Fayth would bite her lip to keep quiet.

Desperate to do something to help Fayth, Glorianna began to form a plan. Seeing a clear space ahead, she slipped her feet from the stirrup. Glancing at Fayth, hoping she would be quiet, she lifted her leg over the saddle. Saying a quick prayer, she jumped from Nina's back. Her feet hitting the hard sand sent a jolt through her body. She swung her arms, fighting a losing battle for balance. Falling to the side, she rolled away from Nina and lay still for a moment to catch her breath.

Dirk whirled around, pulling the horses to a halt. "What are you doing?" he yelled.

She sat up as he jumped from his horse and rushed over to her. He grabbed her arm, jerking her to her feet. The smell of his filthy body revolted her. She clenched her teeth, knowing she had to be strong for Fayth and the baby.

Glaring at him, she snapped, "We have to stop. Fayth is tired and it's almost dark. We can't keep riding in the desert

after dark." She straightened up, attempting to tug her arm free from his grasp.

He grimaced and tightened his hold on her. "You'll do what I say. I've seen for some time you need to be told a thing or two. Your father is too lax with you." Leaning closer, his soft-spoken words sent a chill down her spine. "Now you'll be my woman, and you'll do what I tell you. I've trained many a stubborn mule. I guess I can teach you something."

Dear God, help me think of something. Fayth can't even sit straight in the saddle. If we continue she could lose the baby. Please help us.

Taking a deep breath, Glorianna tried to calm her thoughts. "If we ride in the dark, the horses could walk into a cactus. We can reach the mountains more easily in the morning. We're almost there. Why can't we just spend the night here?"

She forced herself to meet Dirk's gaze as he studied her. Finally, he gave a short nod.

"Get your friend down. We don't have any bedrolls, so you'll have to use the saddle blankets." He released her arm and ran a gritty finger down the side of her cheek. She flinched away and he grinned. "Then again," he said with deadly calm, "maybe Fayth can have the blankets and I'll keep you warm."

Glorianna gasped and stepped away. *God protect me,* she whispered in her soul. *Trust Me,* came the answer written across her heart.

Hurrying to help Fayth, Glorianna shuddered at the thought of Dirk's suggestion. Fayth slipped from the horse and hugged Glorianna. Peering over the horse's back, Fayth turned back to her.

"God can handle this," she whispered. "I know Timothy and the others are following us by now."

"But how will they know where we are? We didn't stay on the road. They won't think to look in the desert for us."

"God knows where we are. He will show them the way," Fayth assured her.

"What are you doing?" Dirk growled. He pulled the horses away and glared at them. When they didn't answer, he spat on the ground. "There won't be any way to cook food. I don't have much anyway. Do I have to tie you or will you stay?"

"Mr. Smith, it's too far to walk. I'm not sure we would find our way from here anyway," Fayth assured him.

He studied her, then led the horses to a tree and tied them securely. Removing the saddles, he carried their blankets back to them. Glorianna spread them out to dry before the night chill set in. A sweaty blanket wouldn't be much of a comfort.

Sinking down by Fayth, Glorianna watched Dirk. In the gathering darkness she could see him studying her. Fear twisted a knot in her stomach. Would he follow through with his threat to keep her warm? What if no one found them? What if Dirk forced her to do something she didn't want? What could she do to stop him? Where was Conlon? She needed him.

She closed her eyes, squeezing tears away. A picture of Conlon swam before her. She could see his black hair, the wayward lock falling across his forehead. She could picture his blue eyes, brightly reflecting his love for her. If there was any way, he would come for her. In her heart she knew how much he loved her. Somehow, he would find a way to get away from Chastity. He had to.

&

Nearing exhaustion, Conlon pulled Champ to a halt. They were less than an hour's ride from Camp MacDowell. In the growing twilight he watched the cloud of dust approaching. The thunder of hoofbeats filled the air. A sense of dread wrapped around him like a mantle.

A few minutes later, his uneasiness grew stronger as he watched the grim faces of the cavalrymen surrounding him. Timothy pushed his horse close to Conlon's. "What are you doing here? Have you seen Fayth and Glorianna?"

Conlon shifted in the saddle. "What do you mean have I seen them?" He wanted to shout his impatience. He needed

to know what was happening.

"They went for a ride this afternoon and haven't returned," Timothy said. "The guard saw them head this direction, but we haven't found them yet."

Forcing his fear away, Conlon replied, "I just rode here from Florence. I haven't seen any sign of them. You're sure they came this way?"

Timothy and several of the others nodded. "We saw fresh tracks on the road. There's no question." Timothy looked torn between fear and anger. "I can't imagine why they would get off the road."

Conlon knew he had to tell him, although he dreaded the reaction. "I might know the reason," he admitted reluctantly. "I'm here because we met a patrol in Florence. They had just come from tracking a criminal to the Superstitions." He paused, looking at the men. "They were tracking Dirk Smith. He killed a man before he escaped and headed this direction. I think he might be after Glorianna."

Timothy paled. "You mean that crazy fool might have Fayth and Glorianna?"

Conlon couldn't speak for a moment, caught in the panic he knew his friend felt. "I hope I'm wrong," he spoke hoarsely. "But I'm guessing he has them."

"What do we do? They could be anywhere." Fear echoed in Timothy's voice.

"I think he'll try to head for the Superstitions. It's the closest place to hide." Conlon turned to look at the forbidding mountains in the distance. "I'll head over there and try to find their tracks."

"I'll go with you," Timothy said. He turned to the others. "The rest of you go back and tell the captain what's happened. He'll probably want to send some of you to help."

"You'll most likely have to wait until morning," Conlon added. "We'll try to leave some sign so you can find us."

When they were alone, Timothy faced Conlon. "Do you think he'll kill them?"

"He won't kill Glory." Conlon hated to think about the women being at Dirk's mercy.

"What about Fayth?"

"I don't know," Conlon answered honestly. "I hope we catch him before he has to make a choice." Deciding to keep silent his fears of what Dirk would do with Fayth when he wanted to be alone with Glorianna, Conlon instead turned Champ toward the mountain range. "Let's ride while there's still daylight. The closer we get, the better our chances of catching them before they disappear in the Superstitions."

They rode until the night drew too close around them, then halted. *Lord, please watch over Fayth and Glory. Be their protection.* The spine-chilling scream of a cougar interrupted his silent plea.

twenty-one

Glorianna took a sip of water from her canteen. Her stomach ached from hunger and fear. They had ridden most of the morning to reach the edge of the mountains. Dirk looked even worse this morning than he had last night. He hadn't slept, probably because he was afraid they would take the horses and run. He had been right. She slept lightly, waking several times during the night, hoping he would be asleep and they could escape. Every time, his eyes were on her, the wicked gleam in them making her uncomfortable.

Dirk turned his horse back to theirs. "You." He gestured at Fayth. Handing her the reins to her horse, he said, "You can go back now. Tell them not to follow us. I've got what I want." He grinned lecherously at Glorianna. "I know she puts on a good show, but she's really glad to go with me. You can tell the captain and Lieutenant Sullivan that."

"I won't leave Glorianna." Fayth nudged her horse closer to Nina.

"Then you'll die," Dirk snarled. He whipped his knife up, lunging at her throat.

Fayth jerked back. Glorianna screamed.

"Now get out of here." At Dirk's command, Glorianna gave Fayth a pleading look. Fayth turned her horse and rode away, glancing back at Glorianna only once.

Dirk nudged his horse next to Nina. "Now it's just the two of us." His rancid breath made her cough. "Let's get lost in these mountains."

He tugged on the reins and Nina followed. Tears filled Glorianna's eyes as she watched Fayth disappear. She felt all her hopes vanish as well. *Trust Me. Lean not on thine own understanding,* a voice whispered.

163

Minutes later, Dirk jerked the horses to a stop. He stared back into the desert and cursed. Glancing behind them, Glorianna could see a rider racing toward them. Her heart beat wildly as she thought she recognized the lean form. It couldn't be, could it?

She nearly fell when Dirk forced the horses to plunge ahead. He turned up a steep slope. Evidently, he thought the rocks would offer shelter. Glorianna loosened her feet in the stirrups. Perhaps she could jump off again. That would give the rider a chance to catch them. One look at the sharp incline they were traveling up convinced her it wouldn't be a good idea. She clung desperately to Nina's saddle, hoping to think of something.

"Get down," Dirk's raspy voice echoed in the stillness.

He dragged her to the rocks, making her climb in front of him. When they were hemmed in on all sides by the huge boulders he pulled her down.

"Smith, you may as well give up. I know you're up there."

Glorianna gasped and tried to rise up. It was Conlon. He had come for her.

"She's mine, Sullivan. She's always been mine."

"If you think she wants you, then why don't you let her decide?" They could hear Conlon working his way up the slope as he talked.

Dirk stood, pulling Glorianna up in front of him. "Stop right there," he ordered. His knife blade flashed in the sunlight. He stuck it under Glorianna's chin, making her tip her head back to avoid the blade. She didn't dare breathe. "If you come any closer I'll cut her. Then neither one of us will have her." His maniacal laughter filled the air.

From the corner of her eye, Glorianna could see Conlon pause. He held his rifle loosely in his hand. She'd seen him on the drills and knew the speed with which he could swing the gun into firing position.

"Let her go, Dirk. She doesn't want you." Glorianna wondered if he felt as relaxed as he sounded. "By now the troops

are on their way. You can see their dust from up there. You won't get away with this."

"I don't know how you found us, but I'm not letting her go. You may as well go and tell the captain. Now get out of here before I hurt her."

While he was talking, Dirk's knife eased away from Glorianna's throat. She lowered her head slightly, getting a better view of Conlon. She watched him open his mouth to reply, then pause, his gaze going to the rocks above them.

"Smith." Conlon's voice lowered. "There's a cougar on the rocks above you."

"Don't try to bluff me." Dirk's knife swept up under Glorianna's chin, forcing her to lift her head again. "Now head on back to your horse and ride out of here."

In the silence that followed, Glorianna strained to look at the rocks above them. The knife blade kept her from turning her head, but she could hear the rattle of tiny rocks sliding down from above. She began to tremble.

"Please, he isn't bluffing."

A low growl above them confirmed her fears. Dirk whirled. His grip loosened. Glorianna dropped to the ground. She could see Conlon swing his rifle up in one smooth motion. Fire and smoke belched from the end of it.

The rifle cracked. The cougar roared. Dirk's frantic scream washed over her. A heavy weight landed on her back, knocking the air from her. In one continuous motion, the body rolled over the top of her and off the rocks. She thought of the long drop to the hillside below and shuddered.

"No!" Glorianna screamed as hands wrapped around her arms, lifting her. She lashed out, struggling to get free.

"Glory, Sweetheart, it's all right." Conlon's soothing voice finally broke through her fear.

Sobbing, she collapsed in his arms. He held her tight, running his hand over her hair. "It's over, my love," he whispered.

"What happened?" Glorianna tried to turn and look over the side of the rocks.

"Don't look," Conlon commanded, pulling her back around. "I shot the cougar, but in its fall it knocked Dirk off the rocks. He's dead, Sweetheart. He won't bother you again."

Glorianna pushed away slightly, tilting her head to look into Conlon's brilliant blue eyes. They were even more wonderful than she remembered. She reached up to brush the lock of hair from his forehead, savoring the touch.

"What happened to Chastity? How did you get here?" She covered her mouth with her hand. "Fayth, she's out in the desert. We have to find her."

He grinned, running a finger down her cheek, tracing the outline of her lips before he answered. "Timothy and I met Fayth. He's taking her back to the camp. She told me where to find you. As for Chastity, the major decided I wasn't the right son-in-law for him. He sent me back to Camp Mac-Dowell for a time."

"For how long?" she asked, fearing losing him again.

"Long enough to get married," he whispered. "That is, if you'll still have me."

"Yes. Oh yes," she breathed as his lips settled over hers in a kiss that made her knees weak.

epilogue

Loud pounding on the door startled Conlon as he scraped the razor across his face. "Ouch!" He winced as a tiny line of red welled up on his jaw.

"Hey, Conlon, you too high and mighty to talk to a friend?" Josiah stuck his head through the door and grinned. "Here you are in the guest-house like you're some high-falutin' fancy pants."

"Can't you knock a little softer? You almost made me cut my throat." Conlon tilted his head and pointed to the blood.

Josiah's laughter rumbled through the room. "If you had your head out of the clouds you would have heard me knock the first two times."

Leaning over the basin to rinse his face, Conlon hoped to hide his embarrassment. Josiah was right. Today was his wedding day, and for the last week or so he couldn't seem to do anything right. Even Champ had been giving him funny looks.

He knew the disorientation had to do with finally getting to be with Glory again. For the past two months he'd been stationed at Fort Lowell in Tucson. Major Denton, true to his promise, had sent Mrs. Denton and Chastity back east for a visit after breaking the news to them that Conlon wouldn't be marrying Chastity.

The major had insisted that Conlon come to Fort Lowell. He wanted him to work as a cavalry liaison officer, acquiring new horses for the troops and making sure they were properly broken. Only the separation from Glorianna marred his happiness. This job was the beginning of his dream. He now had the opportunity to learn where the best horses could be found when he was ready to start his ranch. Glorianna had been very understanding about the separation. She encouraged him in

what she called "their dream," the hope that some day they would have a ranch where they could raise quality horses.

Conlon patted his face dry, taking care not to make the cut bleed again. Did all bridegrooms nick themselves on their wedding day? He grinned at the thought and turned to Josiah. "You're just jealous because I've been writing Glory all those letters instead of sending them to you."

A crooked grin split Josiah's ebony face. "You've got that right. Did you know the mail carrier's horse's legs are two inches shorter than they used to be? Poor thing's been running back and forth between here and Fort Lowell so much he's worn to a frazzle." He slapped Conlon on the back, then sank into a chair. "Speaking of letters, I hear you had an important one waiting for you when you arrived."

Conlon reached into his pocket and pulled out an envelope. For a moment he couldn't speak as emotion made a tight knot in his throat. He ran his fingers over the fine print on the crinkled paper. Even after all these years, he'd recognized his mother's handwriting.

"My mother wrote." He looked up and saw the compassion in Josiah's eyes. "My father died last month. The doctor said his heart gave out."

He pulled out the pages of paper he'd already memorized and opened them up. "Mom says my letter reached them not long before Dad got real sick. She said the news of my becoming a Christian helped them all. Dad's only regret was not getting to see me again before he died. He wanted to tell me how much he loved me and that he forgave me years ago for what happened to my brother."

Conlon leaned forward and rested his elbows on his knees. "You know, I miss Dad, but I've been thinking all night long that now I'll be able to be with him in heaven some day. A few years ago I wouldn't have had that comfort."

Josiah reached over and engulfed Conlon's hands in his callused hands. "I'm glad you wrote them. This will really start the healing. Knowing you're forgiven will help you to

forgive yourself." Josiah stood and stretched. "Now, we'd better get going or you won't be at the ceremony in time. I can't wait until you see your bride in that pretty dress."

"Dress?" Conlon grimaced. "I wanted to bring a special one for Glory. I knew she wouldn't be able to get the right material here, but I couldn't find the time to shop in Tucson. Where did she get a dress?"

"She didn't tell you last night?"

"I got in so late we didn't have much time to talk."

"I'll bet there was time for a kiss or two." Josiah chuckled.

Conlon laughed, feeling his face warm. "That's possible. Now, tell me about the dress."

"Her cousin Kathleen, from back east, sent Glorianna's mother's wedding dress. It came in on a shipment last week. On the same train that brought your letter." Josiah clapped Conlon on the shoulder and steered him toward the door. "Anyway, your bride has been crying ever since. Seems she had given up the idea of having a decent dress to wear for her wedding day."

Thank You, Lord. What a gift for Glory and me. Conlon felt light as air as he followed Josiah outside. He couldn't wait to see Glorianna. When Captain Wilton first insisted he stay in the guest house, he'd objected. Now he was thankful for the privacy he would have with his bride.

≈

"Oh, Fayth, I wish my mother could be here today." Glorianna smoothed her hand over the pure white of her wedding dress. Her mother's dress. The skirt fell in soft folds to her feet. Lace trimmed the long sleeves, the neck, and the hem. The simplicity of the pattern made the dress beautiful.

"Your mother would be so happy for you." Fayth finished the last of the tiny buttons, then came around and gave Glorianna a hug. "I know she'd love Conlon." She took a moment to adjust the lace collar. "Kathleen must be such a blessing to you. I can't believe she even sent these ribbons to weave in your hair. She must have known we would have

no flowers around here."

Glorianna brushed her fingers over her hair. "She is wonderful." She closed her eyes and bit her lip. "Fayth, I'm so nervous my stomach is jittery. I don't think I can do this."

Fayth laughed and hugged her again. "I know just how you feel. I felt the same way right before my wedding. You'll be fine. Ready to go?" She walked around Glorianna one more time as if looking for anything out of place, then gestured to the door.

☙

Conlon held himself stiff, hoping he didn't show any nervousness. Most of the camp had gathered in the dining hall for the wedding. The pastor from Florence had ridden in with him and he waited now with Conlon, watching the door for Glorianna to enter.

The last rays of the sun streamed in as Glorianna stepped through the doorway. In that moment, the golden glow seemed to surround her in a haze. Conlon's chest tightened and he fought for a breath. *Oh, God, she's so beautiful. Thank You for this gift. Please help me to be worthy of her love.*

She glided down the aisle between the rows of people. Her gaze never faltered from his. As she drew closer he could see the silent promise she offered, the promise of her love and commitment for a lifetime.

He stepped forward and joined his hand with hers. With a smile, he returned her promise with one of his own—to love and cherish her forever, just the way God intended.

A Letter To Our Readers

Dear Reader:

In order that we might better contribute to your reading enjoyment, we would appreciate your taking a few minutes to respond to the following questions. We welcome your comments and read each form and letter we receive. When completed, please return to the following:

Rebecca Germany, Fiction Editor
Heartsong Presents
PO Box 719
Uhrichsville, Ohio 44683

1. Did you enjoy reading *Sonoran Sunrise* by Nancy J. Farrier?
   ❏ Very much! I would like to see more books
      by this author!
   ❏ Moderately. I would have enjoyed it more if

   _____

   _____

   _____

2. Are you a member of **Heartsong Presents**? Yes ❏ No ❏
   If no, where did you purchase this book? _____

   _____

3. How would you rate, on a scale from 1 (poor) to 5 (superior), the cover design? _____

4. On a scale from 1 (poor) to 10 (superior), please rate the following elements.

   _____ Heroine   _____ Plot

   _____ Hero   _____ Inspirational theme

   _____ Setting   _____ Secondary characters

5. These characters were special because_____

_____

_____

6. How has this book inspired your life?_____

_____

_____

7. What settings would you like to see covered in future
   Heartsong Presents books?_____

_____

_____

8. What are some inspirational themes you would like to see
   treated in future books?_____

_____

_____

9. Would you be interested in reading other **Heartsong
   Presents** titles?   Yes ❑   No ❑

10. Please check your age range:
    ❑ Under 18   ❑ 18-24   ❑ 25-34
    ❑ 35-45   ❑ 46-55   ❑ Over 55

11. How many hours per week do you read?_____

Name _____

Occupation _____

Address _____

City _____ State _____ Zip _____

"Let your light so shine before men,
that they may see your good works,
and glorify your Father which is in heaven."
MATTHEW 5:16

Introducing a brand new historical novella collection
with four female lighthouse
keepers, at four different points
of the compass in the United
States. Each woman will need to
learn to trust in God and the
guidance of His Light as they
seek to do their appointed tasks.
Salting their characters' lives with
romance, the authors bring each
of these tales to an expected yet
miraculous ending.

When Love Awaits by Lynn A. Coleman
A Beacon in the Storm by Andrea Boeshaar
Whispers Across the Blue by DiAnn Mills
A Time to Love by Sally Laity

paperback, 352 pages, 5 ³⁄₁₆" x 8"

❤ ❤ ❤ ❤ ❤ ❤ ❤ ❤ ❤ ❤ ❤ ❤ ❤ ❤ ❤

❤ ❤ ❤ ❤ ❤ ❤ ❤ ❤ ❤ ❤ ❤ ❤ ❤ ❤ ❤

·······Presents·······

__HP331 A MAN FOR LIBBY, J. A. Grote
__HP332 HIDDEN TRAILS, J. B. Schneider
__HP336 DRINK FROM THE SKY, D. Mindrup
__HP339 BIRDSONG ROAD, M. L. Colln
__HP340 LONE WOLF, L. Lough
__HP343 TEXAS ROSE, D. W.e Smith
__HP344 THE MEASURE OF A MAN, C. Cox
__HP347 THANKS TO A LONELY HEART,
         E. Bonner
__HP348 SOME TRUST IN HORSES,
         S. Krueger
__HP351 COURTIN' PATIENCE, K. Comeaux
__HP352 AFTER THE FLOWERS FADE,
         A. Rognlie
__HP355 LITTLE SHOES AND MISTLETOE,
         S. Laity
__HP356 TEXAS LADY, D. W. Smith
__HP359 AN UNDAUNTED FAITH,
         A. Boeshaar
__HP360 THE HEART ANSWERS, C. Coble
__HP363 REBELLIOUS HEART, R. Druten
__HP364 LIGHT BECKONS THE DAWN,
         S. Hayden
__HP367 LOOK HOMEWARD, ANGEL,
         P. Darty
__HP368 THE HEART SEEKS A HOME,
         L. Ford
__HP371 STORM, D. L. Christner

__HP372 'TIL WE MEET AGAIN, P. Griffin
__HP375 FRIEDA'S SONG, K. Scarth
__HP376 MARK OF CAIN, D. Mindrup
__HP379 NEVER A BRIDE, D. Hunter
__HP380 NEITHER BOND NOR FREE,
         N. C. Pykare
__HP383 LISA'S BROKEN ARROW, R. Dow
__HP384 TEXAS ANGEL, D. W. Smith
__HP387 GRANT ME MERCY, J. Stengl
__HP388 LESSONS IN LOVE, N. Lavo
__HP391 C FOR VICTORY, J. Croston
__HP392 HEALING SARAH'S HEART,
         T. Shuttlesworth
__HP395 TO LOVE A STRANGER, C. Coble
__HP396 A TIME TO EMBRACE,
         L. A. Coleman
__HP399 CINDA'S SURPRISE, M. Davis
__HP400 SUSANNAH'S SECRET, K. Comeaux
__HP403 THE BEST LAID PLANS,
         C. M. Parker
__HP404 AT THE GOLDEN GATE, F. Chrisman
__HP407 SLEIGH BELLS, J. M. Miller
__HP408 DESTINATIONS, T. H. Murray
__HP411 SPIRIT OF THE EAGLE, G. Fields
__HP412 TO SEE HIS WAY, K. Paul
__HP415 SONORAN SUNRISE, N. J. Farrier
__HP416 BOTH SIDES OF THE EASEL,
         B. Youree

Great Inspirational Romance at a Great Price!

Heartsong Presents books are inspirational romances in contemporary and historical settings, designed to give you an enjoyable, spirit-lifting reading experience. You can choose wonderfully written titles from some of today's best authors like Peggy Darty, Sally Laity, Tracie Peterson, Colleen L. Reece, Lauraine Snelling, and many others.

When ordering quantities less than twelve, above titles are $2.95 each.
Not all titles may be available at time of order.

Heartsong Presents
Love Stories
Are Rated G!

That's for godly, gratifying, and of course, great! If you love a thrilling love story, but don't appreciate the sordidness of some popular paperback romances, **Heartsong Presents** is for you. In fact, **Heartsong Presents** is the *only inspirational romance book club* featuring love stories where Christian faith is the primary ingredient in a marriage relationship.

Sign up today to receive your first set of four, never before published Christian romances. Send no money now; you will receive a bill with the first shipment. You may cancel at any time without obligation, and if you aren't completely satisfied with any selection, you may return the books for an immediate refund!

Imagine. . .four new romances every four weeks—two historical, two contemporary—with men and women like you who long to meet the one God has chosen as the love of their lives. . . all for the low price of $9.97 postpaid.

To join, simply complete the coupon below and mail to the address provided. **Heartsong Presents** romances are rated G for another reason: They'll arrive *Godspeed!*